DO THE FUNKY PICKLE

Report to the Principal's Office
Who Ran My Underwear Up the Flagpole?
Do the Funky Pickle

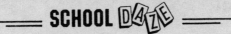
SCHOOL DAZE

DO THE FUNKY PICKLE

JERRY SPINELLI

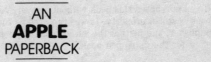
AN
APPLE
PAPERBACK

SCHOLASTIC INC.
New York Toronto London Auckland Sydney

ISBN 0-590-45448-X

23 22 21 20 19 18 17 16 15 14   23/0

Printed in the U.S.A.   40

First Scholastic printing, October 1992

For Jim and Eileen Nechas

DO THE FUNKY PICKLE

1

At precisely 2:35 P.M. the last bell rang through the hallways and rooms of Plumstead Middle School. At precisely 2:35 plus seven seconds, the main door flew open and five eighth-graders tried to be the first to leave. The eighth-graders pulled each other from the doorway and fought like jackels until huge Mr. Hollis, social studies teacher and school bouncer, grabbed them all in his massive mitts and hauled them off to Detention Room. By the time they were seated, the rest of the student body had poured through the doorway.

One of the last to leave was Salem Brownmiller. Long hair and black scarf flying, she pushed and veered and lurched her way through the crowd until, on the sidewalk, she spotted the person she was looking for. "Sunny! Sunny, wait up!"

Sunny Wyler, whom Salem described as her best friend and worst enemy, halted. Salem came

1

rushing up to her, breathless, her eyes wide with excitement. "Sun — " she gasped, and just as quickly Sunny was gone, racing across the street toward a mob of kids yelling on somebody's front lawn.

Salem gave a scornful sigh. As the yelling grew louder, more kids surged forward, practically knocking Salem off her feet. Within moments she was alone on the sidewalk.

Salem had no intention of crossing the street. She folded her arms over her book bag and glared at the revolting spectacle. After a minute or so an old man came out of the house banging on a drum-sized pot with a wooden spoon. No one seemed to notice. Then a second-story window shot open, an old lady leaned out and like a cuckoo started tweeting furiously on a whistle.

That did the trick. The mob broke up, and within seconds the students were once again streaming toward home. The only evidence they left behind was a white scrap of clothing in the middle of the lawn.

Salem did not move. She waited and glared until Sunny trotted over. Now it was Sunny's eyes wide with excitement. "Wow! Great fight. You shoulda seen it."

"No," said Salem stiffly, "I should *not* have seen it. And neither should you. Don't you have any class? Why do you have to join that herd of animals?"

Sunny was baffled. "*Why?* How can you not? Whoever heard of somebody who *doesn't* like to watch a fight?"

"I heard of somebody. *Me!* Why is everybody around here so big on violence? It seems like there's a fight every day. Whatever happened to peace?"

"Peace?" Sunny sneered. "Peace is no fun."

"Oh, really?" said Salem. "Now that's an intelligent thing to say. I guess it's better to watch two hoodlums ripping each other to shreds."

Sunny grinned. "Don't knock it if you haven't tried it."

Salem's lip curled. "You're disgusting."

"You're weird."

"You're revolting."

"You're unnatural."

"You're bloodthirsty."

"You're nice."

"You're — " Salem blinked. "Huh?"

"Gotcha." Sunny started walking.

Salem stood still, sputtering. Sunny always did that, got you all hot and bothered, then — *zap* — she turned it off. It was infuriatingly impossible to win an argument with her, and just as impossible to stay mad at her. In spite of herself, Salem grinned.

She made sure to wipe the grin from her face before she caught up to Sunny. "So," she said, "do you want to hear the big, fantastic, stupendous news or not?"

Sunny merely shrugged. "I already know."

2

Salem's jaw dropped. "You do?"

"Sure," said Sunny. She pulled a Kit Kat mini bar from her pocket and unwrapped it. "I ate sixteen of these for lunch." She popped the bar into her mouth.

Salem stomped. "Get serious."

"I *am* serious. It's a new record."

Salem turned away. "Fine. Then I won't tell you."

The two girls walked on in silence, except for Sunny, who now and then whistled a tune. One block passed. Two blocks. Salem couldn't stand it any longer. She blurted, "Willow Wembley's coming!"

Sunny turned. "What's *that?*"

"The word is *who*. Willow Wembley. The famous author."

Sunny squinted, searching her memory bank. "She write for *Mad Magazine?*"

"Of *course* not!"

5

Sunny shrugged. "Then I wouldn't know her."

Salem squeaked, "Not *know* her? How can you not know her? She writes the best books anybody ever read. She's world famous."

Sunny sniffed, "Never heard of her."

"You never heard of the Klatterfields? Her famous fictional family?"

"Nope."

"You're lying. Tell me you never heard of Clyde Klatterfield."

"Never heard of him."

Salem swooned. "I think I'm going to faint."

"I think I'm going to vomit."

They walked another block in silence. Salem kept staring at Sunny as though she were an alien life-form.

At last Salem took a deep breath and tried again. "Well, anyway, here's what happened. I was walking past the teachers' lounge on my way out of school when I bumped into Miss Comstock. I thought she was just going to say hi, you know, but she took my arm and sort of pulled me over to the side, like this." She pulled Sunny's arm.

"Then she gets this little grin on her face, and she says, sort of whispery, like she doesn't want anybody else to hear, she says, 'Salem, I have a little item of news that might be of interest to you.' She sort of sang it, you know, her voice going up all singsongy?

" 'What is it?' I asked. I was practically dying.

6

"She says, *really* grinning now, 'Willow Wembley is coming to Plumstead.'

"I almost did die. I almost absolutely laid down and croaked right there in front of the teachers' lounge. 'What did you say?' I said.

"She said it again. 'Willow Wembley is coming to Plumstead.'

" '*Here*?' I said. I was hysterical. '*This* Plumstead? Plumstead Middle School?'

"She said yes, in one month. She said there was more news, which I would find even *more* interesting. 'What?' I said. 'What? What?' She said she would announce the rest to her English classes tomorrow. She was just whetting my appetite for now, she said. I *begged* her. 'Please, *please* tell me.' I pleaded. I groveled. But all she would do was smile and pat me on the head and say, 'Just be in class tomorrow,' and then she disappeared into the teachers' lounge. I just stood there, in a coma. I mean, of course, I know why she did it. Miss Comstock knows I'm going to be a writer, so — "

Salem stopped. She sucked in deep breaths, as though she had been underwater. She looked about. She blinked. "What are we doing? Where are we?"

They were standing in a small square room with a tilt-back chair, a gurgling fountain, and a familiar swinging apparatus that made Salem wince just to look at it.

7

"Doctor Morley's dentist office," said Sunny. She was grinning impishly. In another room could be heard the tiny, pointed siren song of a high-speed drill.

Salem gasped. *"What?"*

"Well," said Sunny, "you know how you get when you're worked up. You don't even know where you are. So I figured I'd lead you in here, what the heck."

At that moment a young woman in a starchy white pantsuit appeared in the doorway. "Can I help you girls? I don't believe you have an appointment, do you?"

"Nah," replied Sunny, pulling Salem along. "We were just checking out the place, case we ever got a cavity." She led Salem, whose face was now burning red, past a row of grinning plaster jaws, through the waiting room and outside.

"I don't believe you did that," said Salem.

Sunny made a thoughtful face. "Next time I think I'll take you to the back room of the dry cleaners, check out all those hanging pants and shirts."

Suddenly a noise rang out, like the squawk of a wounded moose: *Ooguh! Ooguh!*

Both girls turned to see Pickles Johnson and Eddie Mott tooling up the sidewalk on the Picklebus, Pickles' green, six-wheeled, surfboard-size skater.

3

The Picklebus slowly circled the girls.

"Hey, Mottster," said Pickles, putting a leer in his voice, "what do you think of these two? Think we ought to offer them a ride?"

"I don't know," said Eddie, playing along. "What if they have boyfriends? We could get beat up."

Pickles looked amazed. "Boyfriends? You kidding? Who would want these two warthogs?"

At that Sunny and Salem charged, knocking the boys from the bus, which went rolling across the dentist's parking lot and into the right front tire of a patient's car. Within moments they were all laughing and Picklebusing down the street.

Salem told the boys of her encounter with Miss O'Malley and of Willow Wembley's upcoming visit.

"*Willow?*" said Eddie. "What kind of name is that? Is she a tree?"

"Does she have a loud bark?" asked Pickles.

"Fun-nee," sneered Salem. "That's what I expected of you two ignoramuses. You're probably still trying to get through *The Little Engine That Could*."

"Is an ignoramus like a hippopotamus?" Eddie inquired.

From the helm Pickles' voice came washing back, "Clyde Klatterfield."

For several seconds there was no sound but the whir of the wheels and their *clack clack* as they crossed the sidewalk cracks.

"Well, well," said Salem, at last, "he reads."

Pickles was always surprising her.

"Hey," said Sunny, "did you guys see the fight?"

"Nah," said Eddie, "we got there too late. Was it good?"

"It was great, man! They were going *bam! pow!*" Sunny jumped from the bus, put up her fists, threw jabs — "*Pow pow pow!*" Threw crosses and uppercuts, punches in flurries — "*Powpowpowpowpowpowpow!*" She ended with an overhand, pummel-fisted, sledgehammer blow to the top of her imaginary victim's head: "*POW!*"

Eddie groaned, "Ohhh, man." He staggered off the bus, wobbled, whirled, and toppled to the ground on his back, arms and legs radiating like wheel spokes.

Pickles stood over him, pumping his arm. ". . . nine . . . ten . . . yerrrrr OUT!" He hoisted Sunny's

10

hand. "The *winnah* . . . and new cham-*peen* . . . from Plumstead Middle School . . . the Plumstead Porkbelly . . . Sluggin' . . . Sunny . . . WWWWWW*Wyler!*"

Three kids cheered and clapped. One kid folded her arms. "Savages," said Salem.

Sunny informed the boys, "Little Miss Muffet is against violence."

Pickles recoiled in mock horror. "Against violence? Nobody's against violence. That's un-American."

Salem stood tall. "Make love, not war."

"What would life be without war?" posed Pickles. "People clobbering each other. Blood and guts. Be honest — wouldn't you like to see an eyeball rolling across the sidewalk right about now . . . like . . . *there*." Something round and blue and glassy fell from Pickles' hand and rolled across the sidewalk.

Salem screamed. The others laughed.

Pickles picked it up. "My lucky marble." He returned the imposter to his pocket.

Salem scowled. "I gave you more credit, Dennis Johnson. I never thought you were bloodthirsty like the rest of them."

Pickles bared his teeth, rolled his eyes, snickered hideously. "Just call me . . . Drrrrracula." He lunged for Salem's throat. Salem screamed, lurched backward, toppled over the Picklebus and took a hard, sudden seat on the cement.

11

Pickles and Eddie helped her to her feet. "See that," said Pickles, "even the Picklebus is violent."

Salem was too furious to see the twinkle in Pickles' eye.

The four Pickleteers rode on home. First off was Salem. Then it was Sunny's turn. As she hopped off the bus and started for her house, Pickles called, "Sun, wait up."

Sunny turned just as Eddie let out a yelp. She did not see the quick kick from Pickles' foot to Eddie's shin that caused the yelp.

"What?" said Sunny.

"Eddie forgot to ask you something."

Sunny turned to Eddie. "So, what?"

Eddie just stared, mouth open, eyes agape, fish-faced.

Sunny waited a few more seconds, then said, "Maserati."

"Huh?" chimed Eddie and Pickles in chorus.

"He was going to ask me what I want for my next birthday, right? I want a Maserati." She ran for her house; at the front door she turned — "Red!" — and went inside.

Pickles shook his head sadly. "You failed, Mottster."

Eddie stared vacantly at the sidewalk. "I can't do it."

"You can do it."

"No, I can't."

"Yes, you can."

"I'm a chicken."

Pickles sighed. "You're a chicken."

He pushed off. The Picklebus rolled down the sidewalk.

4

When they got to Eddie's house, they parked the Picklebus and sat down on the front steps.

"It's not gonna just happen, you know," said Pickles. "You gotta make it happen."

Eddie nodded heavily. "I know . . . I know."

"It's like people say about learning to swim, you just got to dive in and do it. Just do it. Don't think about it."

"I know."

"You think too much."

"Right."

Right, indeed. Think — that's about all Eddie had been doing lately. Think. About Sunny. About how he had met her on the bus on the first day of school and hadn't been able to get her out of his thinker since.

Think: about Sunny in her beloved DEATH TO MUSHROOMS T-shirt.

Think: about Sunny in her Plumstead purple-and-white cheerleader outfit, before she got kicked off for attacking a spectator.

Think: about Sunny in her hamster mascot suit, before she got kicked off that, too, for tackling an opposing football player.

Think think think. Sunny Sunny Sunny. Morning, noon, and night. Rain or shine, the forecast was always the same: Sunny.

And now, with the school dance coming up, Eddie felt a deep push toward action. Before, he had been pretty much satisfied to think about Sunny, dream about Sunny. But now, thinking was not enough. He had to act, do something about it.

He had to ask her to the dance.

But he didn't. He flunked.

"What are you afraid of?" said Pickles. "What do you think she's going to do to you?"

"Do to me?"

"Yeah. I mean, are you afraid she's going to stick her thumbs up your nostrils and pull your nose apart?"

Eddie giggled. "Not really."

"Stick you in boiling fat until you become the world's first french-fried sixth-grader?"

Eddie was laughing too hard to answer.

"So," said Pickles, "if you asked her to the dance, what's the worst that could happen?"

"The worst?"

"Yeah. Seriously."

Eddie thought about it. "Well . . . I guess . . . she could say . . ."

"Say what?"

". . . say . . . no?"

Pickles snapped his fingers. "Bingo. She could say no. Is that going to kill you?"

Eddie knew that here he was supposed to say, *Nah, of course it's not going to kill me.* But the fact was, if she did say no, it *would* kill him.

Pickles read this in Eddie's face. "That bad, huh?"

Eddie shrugged.

Pickles was silent for a while. "Want me to ask her for you?"

Eddie perked up. "Would you?"

"If you want."

Eddie thought, Wow, why didn't I think of that? Sure, why not? He said, "Okay."

Pickles nodded. "Okay." He pushed off on the board. "Gotta go." He rolled out to the sidewalk and turned up the street. He was three houses away when Eddie called, "No!"

Pickles stopped, swung his head. "Don't," called Eddie. "It's not your job. It's mine."

Pickles gave a sharp nod and a thumbs-up sign and pushed off. The wheels sang to him. He smiled. He was proud of his buddy.

Eddie lingered on his front steps, thinking. Tomorrow. It had to be tomorrow, that was clear. Get it over with. Like Pickles said: Dive in.

How do I say it? What words? Hi, Sunny. Would you like to go to the dance with me? Or be cool. Yo, babe. Wanna boogie? And when? At her locker? Coming out of English class?

Something smacked the door behind him. He felt sprinkled on. Rain? He brushed the top of his head; chocolate crumbs flew. The remains of a chocolate cupcake lay at the foot of the door, and out front, at the end of the walkway — where had they come from? — were a handful of nickleheads. As always, the sight of their polka-dot haircuts — the little bald circles — and earrings and leather jackets did queasy things to his stomach.

They were laughing. They had been laughing at him and tormenting him since the first day of school.

"Yo, Mott," one of them called, "come on out and play."

"Bring yer little dollies out. We'll play house."

"Yeah — you can be the mommy and we'll be the daddies!"

"Hah-hah-hah-hah!"

Eddie got up. His knees didn't seem to want to support him. He wished Pickles were here.

"Hey, Mott — look!"

One of them, the one called Cueball, was pulling a yellow marigold out of the little triangular patch at the end of the walkway, pulling it out real slowly, grinning, as though it might scream. He held the flower up by its roots, dangling it, grinning. "You gonna go tell Mommy on me? Huh?"

Eddie went inside, shut the door, threw the bolt. But he could not shut out the grin. It was still there, with him, in his own living room.

5

Salem was far and away the first student into Miss Comstock's English class the next day. The endless hours of last night and this morning had been agony. She pinned her eyes on Miss Comstock, now erasing the blackboard, now sharpening a pencil, now paging through papers on her desk. So casual, so cruel. You would never know by looking at her that she possessed one of the world's great secrets: the rest of the news about Willow Wembley's visit to Plumstead.

The class hadn't even begun, and already Salem wanted to stand up and scream at Miss Comstock: "Stop! I can't take it any longer! Tell me now!" She squirmed and twitched and fidgeted in her seat like a first-grader. If she had her way, she would be running laps around the classroom to ease the tension. She was a balloon swelling with impatience . . . swelling . . . swelling . . .

Pop!

She yelped, "Yaaa!" She looked. It wasn't a pin,

it was Pickles' finger, poking her shoulder, Pickles saying, "A little wound-up there, Brownmiller?"

Salem snarled, "Maybe you'd be a little wound-up, too, if the next couple of minutes were going to be the most important minutes of your life. Now beat it."

Pickles backed away. He looked at Sunny and Eddie. He pointed at Salem, pointed to his own head and made circles with his finger: loony.

The bell rang. Miss Comstock, callously cool, ambled over to the door, looked up and down the hall, and closed the door. She ambled over to her desk, stood in front of it, leaned back against it, gazed over the class, and smiled.

And told them.

She told them that Willow Wembley was coming to Plumstead in one month. Salem heard gasps of surprise. Someone squeaked, "Wow!" Salem felt a burst of pride, since she had already been told, in private.

Miss Comstock went on: "When Miss Wembley comes to our school, she will need someone to accompany her from place to place, someone to guide her and answer questions about the school, and help out if she needs anything. In other words, she will need an escort for the day.

"I have spoken with Ms. Jeffers, the librarian, and we decided that there should be three escorts, not one, and that the escorts should be students."

Her arm, her eyes swept the class. "You. After all, it's your school, you're her readers. So — " Miss Comstock paused, smiled faintly; her eyes seemed to land on Salem for the briefest of moments. "So, here's what we're going to do. This will be a perfect tie-in with our writing program. Everyone will write a short story, no less than three pages, no longer than ten. The judges will choose one story from each grade — sixth, seventh, and eighth. The authors of the three chosen stories will be Willow Wembley's escorts for the full day of her visit to Plumstead Middle School."

Salem slumped in her seat, overcome, knocked out. To be Willow Wembley's escort, her personal escort for the whole day — it was too good to be true, a fantasy. And yet it *was* true, Willow Wembley *was* coming to Plumstead, and one sixth-grader *would* be chosen. Somewhere in the building, in some classroom, at this very moment, was the sixth-grader destined to be blessed above all others. Salem closed her eyes and pressed her writing scarf between her fingers and she knew, absolutely knew, that it had to be her.

The rest of English class was lost on Salem. While the teacher's voice droned on dimly in the background, Salem pictured herself guiding Willow Wembley about the school. ("This is the library, Miss Wembley." "This is the cafeteria, Miss Wembley.") Seeing to her every need. ("Can I get you a cup of coffee, Miss Wembley?") Chat-

21

ting with her writer to writer. ("So, Miss Wembley, what do you think of flashbacks?")

Somewhere a bell was ringing. People were moving. Class was over. Salem gathered her books and drifted out with the crowd, quite unaware of her friends Sunny and Eddie as she passed them in the hallway.

"Look at her," said Sunny. "A zombie."

Eddie nodded. "Yeah."

"She's really going goofy over the Willow Wembley stuff."

"Yeah."

"Probably ought to stay away from her. Safer."

"Yeah."

Sunny turned to Eddie. She stared at him. "So what do you want?"

Eddie flinched. "Huh?"

"You're acting weird."

Eddie shrugged. He looked away from her. He felt his face getting warm, his nose getting itchy. *Do it. Just do it.* He shrugged again. "Well uh . . . I uh . . . I was just . . . uh . . . wondering . . . something." He shrugged. "That's all."

Sunny swung a finger in his face. "Aha! I knew it. You want to ask me something, right?"

Eddie stared at her fingertip. "Well . . ."

"You want to ask me, but you're afraid, right?" She was leaning toward him.

"Well . . ."

She grinned. "I know what it is."

Eddie gaped. "You do?"

"Sure. You want to ask me for one of these. Maybe two." She pulled a plastic sack of Kit Kat mini-bars from her schoolbag.

Eddie stared at the sack of bars swinging before his eyes. The longer he stared, the less sure Sunny felt she was right. She said, "That's not it?"

He winced. He shook his head.

Sunny frowned, thinking. "Hmmm." She looked at Eddie, she looked away, and somewhere in the mob of bobbing heads she seemed to find it. She grinned, she nodded. "So *that's* it."

Eddie stared straight ahead.

"You want to ask me to the dance."

Eddie stiffened, flash-frozen as a fish.

"Well," said Sunny, "go ahead. Ask."

Eddie swallowed. His throat felt like a walnut. *Dive!*

He dived. "Would you go to the dance with me?"

"No," said Sunny brightly and zipped into her next class.

6

There was another fight after school that day, just beyond the last bus waiting in the driveway.

"Be right back," said Sunny, heading for the mob.

Salem lunged, grabbed her. "No!"

Sunny whirled. She stared unbelievingly at the hand grasping her sleeve. "No?"

Salem pleaded, "Sunny, here's your chance to break the habit. Just say no. You don't have to join the rest of the animals. Be an individual."

"I'll be an individual," said Sunny, "an individual animal. Now if you please." She shook her arm. It remained in Salem's grip.

"Sunny, you need help. I'll help you. That's what best friends are for. I'll help you become a decent, nonviolent person."

"If you don't let go," growled Sunny, "*I'll* help *you* become a decent, nonviolent punching bag."

"Sunny, we have more important things to do. We have to talk about my story for Willow Wembley Day."

The mob was screaming.

Sunny drew back her fist. "Let go or I'll slug ya."

Salem laughed. "Be serious."

"On the count of three. One — "

"Sunny — "

"Two — "

"I'm not letting go. I know you would never hit — "

"Three."

She let go.

The two friends stared at each other. Salem's lip was quivering, her eyes gleaming. The mob roared. Sunny turned, looked back at Salem, and took off. After ten steps or so she slowed to a jog, then a walk. She stopped. Her whole body heaved in a single expulsion of breath. She snapped about and came storming back to Salem. "Are you faking it?"

"Faking what?"

"This little blubber act."

Salem sniveled, "No, I'm not faking it. It just so happens I'm an emotional person, especially when my best friend threatens to hit me. Excuse me, I meant to say *slug* me."

"Yeah?" sneered Sunny. "I'm gonna slug you

anyway if you're just trying to make me feel bad so I won't go see the fight."

"Look," said Salem, defiance in her voice. "It's *real*." She squeezed her eyes shut. After several seconds, from the corner of her left eye trickled a solitary tear. She opened her eyes. "See?"

Sunny gave a smirk, winced at the sound of another roar from the mob, and started walking home. Salem came alongside. She looked at Sunny but could not find words. At last she said, "I know that was a really big sacrifice for you to make. You gave up watching a fight for me."

Sunny stared dead ahead, and said nothing.

"I want to say thank you."

Silence from Sunny.

"You must really love me to do that for — "

Sunny snapped, "Brownmiller, if you don't shut your trap, you're still gonna get it."

Salem shut up.

As they neared Sunny's house, Pickles and Eddie rolled up in the Picklebus.

"Hey," said Pickles, "you two see the fight?" He saw the frost in Sunny's eyes. "Don't tell me you missed it. Probably the best fight all year."

Sunny shot all three a final frozen glare and marched into her house.

"What's with her?" said Pickles.

"Oh, nothing," said Salem breezily. "She just decided to give up watching fights. She's against violence now." Pickles and Eddie looked at each other. "Really. She did it because of our great friendship." Salem cast a fond look toward Sunny's front door. "She doesn't want to lose me. Just shows you what can be done."

Pickles and Eddie traded glances that said: *Right.*

Pickles tapped the bus with his green sneaker. "Want a ride?"

"Sure," said Salem. She hopped on and off they went.

When they reached Salem's house, Eddie got off, too. "Gotta talk to Salem about something," Eddie explained. "See you later."

"Later." Pickles waved and was gone.

Salem led Eddie into her house and up to her room. Salem's room looked like Paris. Specifically, the Left Bank of Paris, famous for its artists and writers. Salem had decided that since she could not go to the Left Bank, the Left Bank would come to her. Surrounded by posters and flags and magazines, pictures and berets and, in one corner, a plastic replica of the Eiffel Tower, Salem hoped to draw inspiration for her own writing.

But Eddie was not here to talk of writing. "I need help," he said.

"What with?" asked Salem.

"*Who* with."

"Ah." Salem nodded knowingly. "Sunshine Wyler, alias Sunny."

Eddie sat on the side of the bed, slumped, nodded.

Salem wanted to giggle, for she loved to give advice; but seeing Eddie's dejection, she kept her face serious, counselorlike. She sat on her study chair, crossed her legs, picked up her notepad and pencil and leaned forward. "Tell me about it."

7

Eddie told her about Pickles' advice, and how he had followed it in the hallway after English class, and how Sunny had turned him down. "Turned me down flat," he said, clubbing the mattress with his fist. "So now I'm thinking maybe I shouldn't listen to Pick. Maybe a girl can help me better. Maybe you can figure her out better than a boy and tell me what to do."

It was all Salem could do to keep from shrieking with joy. She jotted down a few thoughts. She looked up at Eddie, arranging her face in an encouraging, confidence-inspiring smile. "Well," she began, "first of all, you're right. Pickles gave you the wrong advice. But that's not surprising. He's only a boy. He doesn't understand women. You can't just go up to a girl like that, out of the blue, and expect her to fall all over you."

Eddie protested, "I wasn't asking her to fall all over me. I was asking her to the dance."

"But you surprised her," Salem pointed out.

"You" — she searched for the word, found it — "*ambushed* her."

"I *asked* her to the *dance!*"

Salem sighed and shook her head. "I know that, but it's *how* you asked her. You went too fast."

Eddie thought about that. "I should talk slower? Like . . ." he spoke as slowly as he could, allowing full seconds between words, even syllables. "Sun . . . ny . . . would . . . you . . . like . . ."

Salem stomped her foot. "No, no, that's not what I mean. I mean you have to, like, build up to it. I mean — " She thought of the love stories she had been reading lately. "I mean romance."

Eddie's face went sour. "Romance? That's grown-up stuff. I'm just a kid. She's just a kid."

Salem launched her finger into the air. "Aha! *That's* the problem. You think of her as a kid."

"Well, isn't she?"

"Compared to a twenty-five-year-old, maybe. But compared to you, no. You ought to be thinking of her as a woman."

Eddie's face was a blank. "A woman?"

"Right."

Eddie turned from Salem and stared vacantly at the wall. In his mind's eye he tried to picture Sunny as a woman. He pictured her with lipstick on, but then he remembered her pretending to flick a boogie ball at him in math class. He imagined her wearing high heels, until he remembered her DEATH TO MUSHROOMS T-shirt.

He turned back to Salem, shook his head sadly. "I can't do it."

Salem reached out and patted him on the hand. "That's okay. I understand. It's not your fault."

"What are you talking about?"

"I mean, it's not your fault that you're a boy, and there are some things that boys can't understand."

"We're stupid?"

"No, just immature. Girls mature much faster than boys. It's a scientific fact."

"It is?"

"Sure. Why do you think little girls play with dolls?"

Eddie was stumped. He knew that's what little girls did, but he had never asked himself why they did it.

Salem answered her own question. "Because they're getting ready to have families. Even when they're only two years old. And what do you suppose boys are doing when they're two?"

Eddie thought, tried to remember all the way back to when he was two. "Dump trucks?"

Salem folded her arms and grinned with great approval, as though she were a teacher and he had just given the perfect answer. "Exactly. See?"

No, as a matter of fact, he didn't see, but obviously Salem saw, plus probably the rest of the world, so he nodded. He made a mental note to ask his father some day what was wrong with dump trucks.

"You see," Sunny went on, "it takes boys a long time to grow up. Much longer than girls. You boys . . ." She wagged her head and smiled in faint wonder. "You boys . . . " She stared at him, squinting as if through a telescope over the pink eraser end of her pencil.

Eddie began to feel uncomfortable. Was his fly open? He checked. No. "What are you looking at?"

"Oh," she mused, "you. In the future."

"Huh?"

"I'm seeing you, oh, about two years from now. Eighth-grader."

"Really?"

"Yep."

"What do you see?"

She squinted, squinted. "An earring."

Eddie squawked. "Never!"

Salem nodded matter-of-factly. "Oh yes. You'll see other stud boys wearing them and you'll have to play follow-the-leader and get one yourself. Typical immature boy behavior."

Eddie asked, "What else?" not sure he really wanted to know.

Salem ticked them off on her fingers. "Oh, you'll turn into a bully, squashing little sixth-graders like you get pushed around now. Then you'll start

32

acting like a big macho he-man. You'll call girls chicks. You'll smoke a cigarette. You'll say bad words. You'll get your driver's license and pester your parents for the car, and then you'll crack it up. You will write stuff on bathroom walls."

"What stuff?" said Eddie.

"Hah!" Salem snorted with contempt, cleverly disguising the fact that she had no idea what he might write. She sneered distastefully at him. "You'll find out soon enough."

Eddie felt overwhelmed, smothered, drowning in a tidal wave from his own future. How did she know what lay ahead for him? And Sunny, in the hallway that morning, she had said, "You want to ask me to the dance." What was it with these girl people? He had heard about a mysterious something called women's intuition. Was this it? He felt weak, empty, small, powerless, dumb. He saw before him a lifetime that had already been predicted by the females around him. Like at every step into the future, they would already be there, waiting for him, snickering, wagging their fingers.

It was all too scary, too heavy to think about, so he turned his back on it and found himself staring at the question he should have asked in the first place: "What's all that have to do with me asking Sunny to the dance?"

Salem stared at him. Frankly, she didn't know either. She consulted her notes. Ah, there it was, the word of words. "Romance, of course," she said, her arched eyebrows daring him to ask another silly question.

At that moment a call came from Salem's mother downstairs: "Salem! Dinner!"

Eddie glanced at the clock radio. Dinnertime for him, too. He popped up from the bed and clattered down the stairs behind Salem.

On the way home Eddie felt more baffled than when he had entered Salem's house. That night, while taking his bath, he stared at the pink square tiles above the tub. *You will write stuff on bathroom walls.* He closed his eyes. He searched his innermost self, trying to detect the beginnings of an urge to write there. But all he could feel was the soft crinkle of Mister Bubble soapsuds against his skin.

8

When Sunny boarded the school bus next morning, she still looked grumpy from missing the fight the day before. She took a seat way up front and never even looked back at Eddie.

Meanwhile, Eddie was forced to watch a pair of eighth-graders kissing in the seat directly in front of him. Eddie was sitting on an aisle seat, so he couldn't just look out the window. He had little choice but to stare straight ahead, and when he did so there were these two faces about twelve inches away. Only half of each face was presented to him: one eye, one ear, half a nose, half a mouth. It reminded him of those paintings on Egyptian tombs, where everybody is shown from the side, in profile.

To make matters worse, they were nicklepeople. He was a nickelhead, she a nicklechick, as the girlfriends of nickleheads were called. Eddie would have felt safer if the seat were occupied by a fifteen-foot alligator.

The nickelhead wore a skull and crossbones earring. The nickelchick wore a nose ring, a little gold thing poked right through the flared flap of her nostril. It made Eddie cringe, and yet he could not take his eyes from it. He wondered if there was another ring on the far side of her nose.

As with all nickelheads, the boy's haircut featured quarter-sized bald circles polka-dotted over a teddy-bear-cut scalp. He also featured about the fattest, ripest zit Eddie had ever seen. It squatted an inch from the side of the kid's mouth, like a miniature, yellow-headed volcano about to erupt.

The girl's hair was bluish-green. To Eddie it looked as if she had dunked her head in Easter egg coloring. The style was two inches tall flat-top — flat enough to lay a tablecloth on — except for the back center. There a stiff, gloppy spike pointed straight at the ceiling, like an aqua javelin. Her lipstick was the same color as her hair.

They smooched and snuffled and nuzzled and whispered things that Eddie, close as he was, could not make out. Suddenly, in the middle of a nuzzle, the nickelhead's one visible eyeball shifted all the way to the left, till it was staring straight at Eddie. The nickelhead pulled back, turned full-face, and snarled, "Wadda *you* lookin' at?"

"Nothing," said Eddie. His eyes reached out and clutched the back of a boy's head two rows up and across the aisle.

"You lookin' at us?"

Eddie shook his head briskly. "No."

The nickelchick giggled. "He was."

The nickelhead looked at her, looked at Eddie. He grinned. He nodded. "Yeah. You *was* lookin', right?"

Eddie slammed his head from side to side. "Not me."

The grin vanished. "Yeah, you was lookin' okay — at *her*."

An icepick of terror pierced Eddie's heart. "No!"

The nickelhead flinched backward, he frowned. "No? Waddaya mean no? You wasn't lookin' at her?"

"No."

"Why not?" His face came over the seat top, inches from Eddie's. "She too ugly for ya to look at?"

Eddie tried to speak; nothing came out. He cleared his throat, he swallowed. "No . . . no . . ."

"No what?"

"No . . . she's not ugly."

The girl was giggling.

"Look at her," commanded the nickelhead.

"Huh?"

"*Look* at her."

Eddie's head stayed still while his eyeballs

crawled to the far corners of his eyes. They saw her face loom larger and her lips purse and pucker until she looked like some giant painted tropical guppy. The blue-green lips blew him a kiss.

"My chick ugly?" came the nickelhead's voice.

"No."

"What is she then?"

"Not ugly."

"Tell her."

"Huh?"

"Tell her. Look at her" — Eddie felt his head sandwiched by a pair of hands and swiveled till he was facing the tropical fish — "and tell Angelpuss what she is."

Anglepuss puckered and blew him another kiss. She batted her long black eyelashes. She reached out and tweaked his cheek. "Hiya, cutie."

Eddie gulped, gulped again. "She's . . . uh . . ."

"No, *no*," snapped the nickelhead. "Tell *her*. Say *you're*."

"You're — " The word came out like the squeak of a rusty mouse. Eddie cleared his throat. "You're . . . uh . . . buh . . . beautiful."

Angelpuss squealed. "Ouuu!" She tweaked his cheek again. "Thank, you, cutie."

Eddie relaxed a little, thinking, It's over. But the girl's smile became suddenly a scowl. She turned to the boy. "He's lying. I'm not beautiful."

She stroked her spike, she batted her lashes. "I'm *gorgeous!*"

They laughed. Eddie stopped relaxing. His peripheral vision revealed the other riders sitting nearby, many of them fellow sixth-graders, all of them ramrod rigid, staring straight ahead. No one to mess with a nickelhead, no one to save him.

"So, Puss, what's the punishment for lying?" The nickelhead was speaking to the nickelchick but was grinning at Eddie.

"Gee, Weasel, I don't know. Let's think about it."

The two of them put on frowns, thinking. Suddenly the girl piped, "Ah!" She grabbed her boyfriend's chin and turned his face toward her. Her eyes lit up. "Yes. Firing squad." She tugged on the nickelhead's head till he was leaning well over the back of his seat. She positioned his face a mere six inches in front of Eddie's face.

"Ready"

She fine-tuned the nickelhead's face so that Eddie was staring dead into it.

"Aim."

By the time she yelled "Fire!" Eddie was gone, racing down the aisle. He might well have crashed through the front of the bus had it not just then come to a stop and opened its door to the school. Eddie flew outside, past the goggled eyes of

39

Sunny Wyler. He did not stop till he was safely at his desk in homeroom.

Later that morning, on the way to English class, Eddie still felt a little shaky. Salem breezed up to him and said, "I have something for you." And he knew, by the lilt in her voice and the twinkle in her eye, that it had to be good.

9

Salem slipped the piece of paper to him while Miss Comstock was reading aloud to the class a chapter from Willow Wembley's latest book about the Klatterfields, *The Owl Hoo Came to Dinner.* Eddie unfolded the paper. It was a letter, typed very neatly, a grown-up-looking job. He read it:

Dear Sunny,

Please forgive me if I offended you by asking you to the dance. I did not mean to offend you or make you angry.

Nevertheless, I accept full responsibility for my actions, and if you are upset in any way, then I am to blame.

But what else am I to blame for? Ah, that is the question!

Am I to blame for thinking about you morning, noon, and night?

Yes.

Am I to blame for all the wild and peerless feelings that swirl through my being like a whirlpool of emotion whenever my eyes behold you?

Yes.

Am I to blame for wanting to take you in my arms and sweep you across the dance floor to the melodies of love songs and swirling lights at the school dance on Friday, November 16th, at 7:30 P.M.?

Yes! Guilty as charged!

Yes! Yes! Yes!

When I see you walking down the hall . . .

It went on and on like that, three full pages, single-spaced. The bell was ringing as he reached the end:

> *Most truly yours,*
> *Your Faithful Admirer*

Salem nudged him on the way out. Her eyes were bright. "Well?"

Eddie looked at her. "Well what?"

She tapped the three pages in his hand. "What do you think of it?"

Eddie stared at the letter. In truth, he did not know what to think. With all its twists and turns and flowery words, the letter itself was a swirling

42

whirlpool. One thing for sure, Eddie could never have written it. Nor, he guessed, could Pickles.

But then, he didn't really have to understand it, did he? All he had to do was put himself in Salem's hands. She was the one who understood girls. She must know what she was doing. So he nodded and said, "Pretty good."

Salem beamed. "Yep. I think so, too, if I do say so myself. The secret is romance. Remember that word. Never forget it." She stared at him, confirming that he was remembering. "Okay, now, the first thing you do is sign it, in your own handwriting."

"Then do I mail it to her?"

Salem thought. She shook her head slowly. "No, I don't think so. I think it would be more romantic for her to find it. You know, where she least expects it."

"So where's that?"

Salem thought some more. "How about a book?" She tapped Eddie's math book. "Wouldn't that be something? She's in math class and she opens her book and what does she see — a letter. From a boy." Salem's eyes rolled upward, picturing it. "Yes! That's it."

Eddie slipped the letter between the pages of his math book. "Then what?"

"Then we wait and see. If you want my personal opinion, I think she's going to be in the throes of rapture."

43

Eddie frowned. "What's that?"

Salem tossed her hand. "Oh, just a romantic phrase. It means she'll probably start calling you on the phone and walking past your house and writing stuff in her looseleaf."

This was interesting. "Yeah? Like what?"

"Oh, like your name, about a million times. Like hearts that say 'S.W. Loves E.M.' Like 'Mrs. Edward A. Mott.'"

Eddie reacted as if he had been slapped. "Hey, who said anything about getting married?"

Salem patted his hand. "Calm down, boy. Listen, you hired me to help you, didn't you?"

"Yeah."

"Okay. Number one, I'm a writer, so it's my job to understand human nature. Number two, even before I was ever a writer I was a girl, which is why you came to me in the first place. Right?"

Eddie nodded.

"Okay. So trust me. Okay?"

Eddie nodded again.

Kids were running. Next class was about to start.

Salem waved. "After she gets the letter, we'll have a meeting." She darted into a classroom.

The hall was almost empty. Eddie hurried. He reached math just as the bell rang.

Doors closed up and down the hallway. A single student remained. It was Cueball, the nickelhead. He had been walking behind the shrimpy Mott kid

44

and the girl. He had intended to hassle Mott when he noticed the sheets of paper sticking from his book. So instead he pulled the sheets out. And now, in the silent hallway, he stopped to read them.

10

"It's gone," said Eddie. His eyes were wide with disbelief, his face in pain. "It's *gone*."

"How?" said Salem. "I saw you put it in your book."

"I don't know. It's not there now. I don't know."

They were outside the building for gym. It was a mixed class: boys and girls, sixth-, seventh-, and eighth-graders.

"Well, you look until you find it," Salem grumped.

"What if I don't? You can write me another one, can't you?"

Salem stopped, put her hands on her hips. "Eddie, do you know what it took to write that? I was inspired. It was like the muse of romance was dictating it to me. My fingers were flying."

"Didn't you save it on your computer?"

"No. I didn't *do* it on my computer. Whenever my subject is romance, I use an old-fashioned pen, the kind you have to keep dunking in an inkwell.

I only typed it up because Sunny would recognize my handwriting."

The gym teacher blew his whistle, time to start. The game was football, tail football. The teacher handed out bright red strips of cloth. Each student stuck one end into the back of his or her gym shorts, so everyone had a "tail." The idea was to pull the tail from the ball carrier.

"Here," said Salem to Eddie, "you take it." She was holding out her red strip.

"It's your tail," said Eddie. "Put it on."

Salem snickered. "Are you kidding? I don't wear tails. Do you really think I'm going to go running around with a red tail sticking out behind me? It's bad enough I have to wear these dumb clothes in the first place."

"But it's only gym class," said Eddie. "That's all it is."

Salem lifted her chin. She thrust the cloth strip at Eddie. Eddie sighed, shook his head, and accepted it. He balled it up and stuffed it into one of his shorts pockets.

Salem and Eddie were on the same team. The other side started out with the ball. On the first play the quarterback threw a pass to a girl, who came running with the ball straight toward Salem. Salem stepped aside, and the girl dashed on by for a touchdown.

A girl came charging over. It was Angelpuss, the nickelchick. Her hair spike was orange now.

"Hey!" she yelled at Salem. Salem turned. The nickelchick jammed her face up to Salem's. "Waddaya think you're doing?"

Salem's eyebrows rose. "I beg your pardon?"

"Why didn't you stop her? Why didn't you pull her tail."

Salem sniffed. "I do not *wear* tails, and I do not *pull* tails."

"Yeah?" snarled Anglepuss. "Well, pull *this*." She reached behind, yanked out her own tail and flapped it in Salem's face.

Eddie stepped forward. "Hey!"

Somebody called, "Fight!" The gym class converged.

"Hey *what*?" came a familiar voice behind Eddie. He turned. It was Angelpuss's boyfriend, whom she had called Weasel.

Weasel took the red tail from Angelpuss and dusted Eddie's face with it. "You got a problem?"

Eddie backed off, spread his arms. "No . . . no problem here."

At that point the gym teacher waded into the crowd. "All right, break it up. You can fight when we get to boxing."

The game resumed, with Eddie, Salem, and Angelpuss on one team, Weasel on the other. Whenever Weasel's team had the ball, they would run plays straight at Salem. Time after time Salem stepped aside, like a matador waving a bull by. Angelpuss was getting madder and madder.

Eddie had his own problems. Offense or defense, wherever he lined up, there was Weasel, squarely opposite him, grinning. He kept trying to goad Eddie into a confrontation. Weasel was the only member of his team who did not carry the ball straight for Salem. Instead, he ran straight at Eddie, and Eddie ran the other way. "Come on! Come on!" called Weasel. He even turned his rear end toward Eddie and flapped his tail. "Here I am. Stop me."

Eddie wasn't biting. A long time ago he had decided to steer clear of all nickelheads. When Eddie's team was on offense, he refused to be a ball carrier, and he never ran out for a pass. Meanwhile, Weasel brayed across the line, "Give it to Mott! Give it to Mott!"

Since the gym teacher was always hanging around nearby, things never really got out of hand. But then the teacher was called into the school building to answer a phone call. "I'll be right back," he told the class. "Don't kill each other."

Weasel sidled up to Eddie and whispered, "He didn't say don't injure each other."

Eddie's team had the ball. The quarterback threw a pass to Angelpuss. Eddie settled back to watch the nickelchick dart this way and that to escape the tail chasers, all the while laughing and shrieking.

Then Eddie noticed something strange was happening. As Angelpuss was fleeing her chasers, she was not running toward the goal line. She was racing in loops and squiggles that, as it happened, carried her closer and closer to Eddie. With the action coming in on him, Eddie started backing away, but he was too late. By the time he realized what was going on, Angelpuss was charging full speed at him and shrieking, "Here — catch!"

The ball came flying. Instinctively — and stupidly — Eddie caught it. And just like that, Weasel was on him.

From the first instant it was clear that Weasel had no intention of bringing the matter to a quick conclusion by pulling out Eddie's tail. He mauled and pawed Eddie, pulling his shirt, his shorts, his arms, his legs, his ears. He kneaded Eddie like a lump of bread dough, twisted him like a pretzel, practically turned him inside out, all the while croaking, "Hey, where's that tail? Can't find that tail!"

Eddie yanked it out himself. "Here it is!" But Weasel just stuffed the red strip into Eddie's waistband and went on mauling him.

Even for a peacemaker such as Salem, this was too much. "Let him go, you brute," she commanded.

Weasel looked up in surprise, but it was Angelpuss who acted. "You calling my boyfriend a brute?" she growled, and with a sideways swipe of her hip sent Salem reeling backward and onto the grass.

Now it was Eddie's turn. With Weasel momentarily distracted, he pulled himself free and headed for the nickelchick. "Hey!"

Angelpuss met him halfway, hands on hips, chin out. "Hey *what*, turtle turd?" She moved so close to him that the tip of her nose was touching his. Her feet were on his sneakers.

Eddie's voice dried up in his throat; he swallowed several times; his nose twitched; his ears reddened. "Hey . . . stop," he rasped.

"Watta you gonna do if I don't?" she said. Eddie had no answer. "You gonna *bop* me?" She took one step back. "Huh?"

Eddie gulped. "I don't hit girls."

She laughed. She looked around at the gaping, expectant faces. She grinned at Weasel. "Okay then — I'll bop you." She dropped her arms to her sides, lowered her head and darted forward. The top of her forehead caught Eddie square in the nose.

Eddie staggered backward. It felt like a pumpkin had been stuffed up his nose. Faces floated in the tears springing from his eyes. He was sure his nose was broken, yet there didn't seem to be any blood.

And now the gym class was erupting, going bonkers, because here was not only a fight, but the rarest fight of all: a girl versus boy fight. Few kids in the history of the human race had been privileged to witness such a spectacle.

"Go, Mott!" they shouted. "Go, Angelpuss!"

They were behind him, pressing him, pushing him forward, toward the girl with the orange spiked hair. And then they were falling away, letting him go, because the teacher was returning, trotting across the field, blowing his whistle, telling them all to get inside *now*! And for a brief second, as the others streamed by, Eddie was left alone with the girl. He blinked and blinked again, trying to clear the blur from his eyes, to see if she was coming at him again. She wasn't, she was just standing there.

He turned and ran into school.

11

After school that day, Sunny headed for the lobby to feed Humphrey, the Plumstead hamster and mascot. Before she even reached the glass tank, she noticed something new inside: a piece of paper. She raised the cover screen and took it out. One edge was ragged from where Humphrey had snacked. She unfolded the paper. It was a letter. Typewritten. To her.

She read it.

Outside, Pickles and Salem were at the Picklebus. Salem was telling Pickles about gym class that day. "Barbarians. That's all I see around me. Even the girls. You should have seen the way that . . . that female, pardon the expression, attacked Eddie. And the rest of them! The bloodthirsty looks on their faces. Screaming for murder. I shudder to think what would have happened if the teacher hadn't come back." She stopped, thought, shuddered. "What's the world coming to?"

Pickles, who had been content to listen, was caught off guard. At the end of a long day in school, he really wasn't ready to think. So he just waited, knowing Salem would answer her own question. She did. "I'll tell you what the world's coming to. It's coming to the end. *Finito.* You know what we're probably looking at here?" Pickles looked around. "We're probably looking at the end of civilization as we know it."

Pickles looked again, seeking clues to civilization's collapse. Just then, not ten feet away, one boy sneaked up behind a second boy and knocked his books to the ground.

"Hey," growled the second boy, "pick them up."

"I'll pick 'em up," grinned the first, "after you pick *that* up." He spit on the ground.

"See what I mean," said Salem, turning away in disgust. "Some day the history books will say it all started right here in Plumstead Middle School."

Eddie showed up.

"How's the nose?" said Pickles.

Eddie touched it. "A little sore, but okay."

"You shouldn't have stuck up for me," Salem told him. "You should have stayed out of it."

"She pushed you," Eddie countered.

"That's no excuse. Just because she was being

a barbarian doesn't mean you should be, too."

"But what if she pushed you again? What if she didn't stop?"

Salem gave a dismissive wave of the hand. "That's okay. I believe in nonviolence. I do not believe in striking back."

"Not even if she punched *you* in the nose?" said Pickles.

Salem sniffed. "Not even."

"Not even if she pulled your hair out till you were bald? Not even if she pulled your ears like bubble gum and tied them together behind your head? Not even if she pulled off your shoes and socks and let ten lobsters clamp on every one of your toes?"

Eddie was howling, Salem was scowling. "Some day, Mister Johnson, you'll learn some things are not funny."

"But, Salem," said Eddie, "you did the same thing I did. You stuck up for me."

Salem looked away. "That's different."

"Different? How?"

"I'm a woman. Women don't have to explain themselves." She tossed her writer's scarf over her shoulder and boarded the Picklebus.

The three of them coasted toward the main entrance. Sunny was coming out. She was smiling, but the smile had a tilt to it.

"Yo, Picklepeople," she called brightly. She

waved a plastic bag in the air. "Mini Kit Kats! Who wants some?"

Three kids answered, "I do!"

"Hands out," Sunny directed.

Three hands shot out, palms up.

Sunny dipped into the bag, pulled out a mini-bar, put it in Salem's hand. "One for you." She put one in Pickles' hand. "One for you." A second in Salem's hand. And Pickles' hand. Salem. Pickles. Salem. Pickles.

All eyes but Sunny's were staring at Eddie's upturned hand, still bare.

Sunny doled out the last two bars to Salem. "For you and . . ." — to Pickles — "for you."

No one moved, no one spoke. Only Sunny smiled her tilted smile.

At last Pickles said, "Didn't you forget somebody?"

For the first time Sunny looked directly at Eddie. Her eyes shot open as if in surprise. "By golly, you're right!" She reached into her pocket, pulled out a balled-up piece of paper and dropped it into Eddie's hand. "Here, you can eat this."

"Have a nice day," she said breezily and whisked herself away.

Eddie uncrumpled the paper. He began to read. A bewildered expression came over his face. He looked up. "What's this all about?"

Salem took the letter. She scanned it, then began to read aloud:

Dear Sunny,

I am writing this letter to tell you how beautiful you are. Your eyes are like pools. Cesspools. Your ears are like flowers. Cauliflowers. Your nose is as cute as a button. A bellybutton. Your teeth are like stars. They come out at night. Your lips are like cherries. They're the pits. You have the best shape I have ever seen. On an elephant. As you can see I am just crazy about you. I am also just crazy. Will you go to the dance with me?

Your lover boy,
Eddie Mott

12

The three friends stared at each other.

"I didn't write this," said Eddie.

"It's a fake, " said Salem. "Somebody is framing you."

"The *real* note!" piped Eddie. "*That's* what happened. Somebody stole it and then did this."

"Who?" said Pickles.

Eddie didn't have to think for long. "A nickelhead, I bet. Almost everything bad that's happened to me this year, a nickelhead had something to do with it."

Pickles took the letter from Salem. He looked it over. Sunny was already two blocks away. "Let's go after her."

"All aboard!" called Pickles. Pickles tooted the picklehorn and the green six-wheeler zoomed down the driveway. They caught up to Sunny as she was turning a corner. She kept staring straight ahead. The bus rolled alongside.

"Sunny," said Salem, flapping the letter, "did

you read this thing? You don't really believe Eddie wrote it, do you?"

"Somebody wrote it."

"But not Eddie."

"His name is on it."

"It's forged. That's why — look — his name is typed instead of written, so you can't tell it's not his handwriting."

"That's crazy. Who would write a letter for him?"

Salem hesitated, recalled that's exactly what she had done. "Who knows? Anybody. Somebody playing a joke on him. Somebody trying to get him in trouble."

The wheels of the green board hummed as they kept pace with Sunny. Eddie cleared his throat. "I have enemies."

Salem echoed, "He has enemies."

Sunny snorted. "I'm impressed."

Salem jammed her foot to the sidewalk, halting the bus. "Sunny, stop!"

Sunny took two more steps and stopped. She continued to stare stiffly down the street.

"Sunny, you *know* he didn't write it, because you *know* he likes you. Everybody knows it."

Eddie looked around. He felt his face getting warm. Was Salem right? Did everybody know it?

Sunny turned. Her eyes skipped over Eddie and landed on Salem. "I am not an elephant." She walked on.

59

Salem jumped from the Picklebus and ran after her. "Sunny, you can't treat Eddie like that."

Sunny smirked. "Really?"

"No." Salem held out a handful of Kit Kats. "If you're not giving these to Eddie, you're not giving them to us."

In the background Pickles uttered, "*Us?*"

"Fine," said Sunny. She held out the empty plastic bag. "Fork 'em over."

Salem gaped. Then she rushed back to Pickles, snatched the mini-bars from his hand and dumped both his and hers into the plastic bag.

Sunny waved the bag and took off. "Have a nice life."

Salem stood stunned. The bus rolled up to her. "Let's walk," said Pickles. A few nights before, Pickles had screwed a metal post onto the front of the board and fastened a length of clothesline to it. Now he unwrapped the rope and started pulling the board behind him like a pet on a leash.

They walked a block and a half before Salem fumed, "Ouuu, that girl. Sometimes I want to . . ."

"Don't sweat it," said Pickles.

"Don't *sweat* it? How can I *not* sweat it? How am I supposed to write my story for Willow Wembley with all this going on? I need to clear my mind. I need peace and quiet. So what do I get? I get nickelheads and loony tunes and bloodthirsty savages and now a best friend who treats me like dirt."

Pickles said matter-of-factly, "She didn't mean it."

Salem's eyebrows went up. "Oh, really?" Being the writer, Salem considered herself the group's expert on human nature. "You have it all figured out, I suppose."

"Sure." Pickles pulled a Kit Kat from his pocket and unwrapped it.

Salem screeched. "I gave them back to Sunny!"

"Not this one." Pickles held it out. "Want it?" Salem just glared. "Guess not. Mottster? Open." Eddie opened his mouth, Pickles stuck it in. "She knows he didn't write the letter."

Salem scoffed. "Is that so, Doctor Johnson? Well, pray tell, explain it to us poor ignoramuses."

"Simple. The letter hurt her feelings. She had to blame someone. Eddie's name was on it. She blamed him. Just his bad luck."

"Oh, sure," snickered Salem. "Sunny getting hurt feelings? Sunny caring that somebody calls her an elephant? May I remind you that this is the person who once went sixteen days without washing her hair. May I remind you that this is the person who wears a DEATH TO MUSHROOMS T-shirt till it rots off her back. And you think she cares what she looks like? You better go back to school, doc-*tor*."

Pickles shrugged. "Just an idea. Anyway, she'll get over it. Probably call you up tonight, like nothing ever happened."

Salem made a mocking laugh. "Hah-hah. Thank you, Doctor. Is there anything else you can do to straighten out my life?"

"Sure," said Pickles casually, "maybe I could help you with your story."

Salem nearly popped. "Hah! That's the funniest thing I've heard all day. Pardon me for not laughing. Good-bye." She crossed the street and headed home.

Salem ate two bites of dinner and went up to her room. She planted herself at her desk to begin making notes for her story. After ten minutes she slammed her ballpoint pen down on a still blank sheet of paper. It was no use.

The phone rang. She picked it up. The voice was Sunny's, bright, snappy. "Yo, pickleperson."

Like nothing had happened.

13

"I need moves," Eddie said.

"Moves?" said Salem. "What moves?"

"You know, moves. To get girls."

"Oh. *Those* moves."

It was two days before the dance. They were in Salem's room after school.

"I guess we don't want to try another letter, do we?" said Salem.

Eddie shot back, "No more letters."

Salem paced about the room. "Okay, moves . . . moves . . ."

"I figure this way," said Eddie. "She's not going to the dance with me, no matter what I do. So forget that, right?"

"Right."

"So how about the dance itself? Is she going?"

"If I have to drag her by her hair."

"Okay. So I need some moves I can pull at the dance."

Salem nodded. "Right." She paced, paced.

"Moves . . . moves . . ." She stopped, turned, studied him for a moment. "You have to change."

"Change?"

"Yes. Be different. The dance will be different, for her anyway. I don't think she's ever been to one. Music. Low lights. Boys. It'll be new. You should be new, too."

Eddie thought it over. "One thing for sure, the old me isn't getting anywhere."

Salem clapped her hands. "Exactly! So . . . what can we do?"

Eddie was sitting on the edge of the bed. Salem stood before him, hands on hips, studying him with squint-eyed intensity. She flicked a forefinger. "Stand." Eddie stood. She twirled her finger. "Turn." He turned. "Walk." He walked.

A smile crept over Salem's face. She nodded slowly. "It's the walk."

Eddie, who had reached the far wall, turned. "The walk?"

"Yep. You walk like, well . . . walk some more."

He walked across the room and back.

Salem nodded decisively. "You walk like a wimp."

"But I *am* a wimp," Eddie blurted.

"Makes no difference," she said. "We're not working on what you *are*. It's your image."

She was losing him. "What are you talking about?"

"Impressions. Look, the real problem is, Sunny

doesn't know what a great guy you are. Why? Because all she sees is a wimp. You have to show her somebody else."

"You mean pretend to be somebody else?"

"Sort of."

"Okay, so suppose I pretend to be somebody else. Then she starts to like me, right?"

"Right."

"Okay, so she starts to like me — and *then* she finds out that underneath this new pretend me, I'm still the same old wimp shrimp Eddie Mott I always was. Big deal."

"Maybe so, but this time she'll *like* the same old Eddie." She leaned in and wagged her finger. *"Because she liked your moves."*

Eddie thought about that. He pictured Sunny liking him. He nodded firmly. "Okay. Teach me to walk."

Salem placed him against the wall. She tried to imagine how the men in romantic stories would walk. "Okay, something like this." She demonstrated. "See . . . head up . . . shoulders back . . . no shuffling . . . lift your feet . . . step out, like a man."

Eddie gave it a try.

Salem screeched. "No, no! You look like a walking mannequin. Not so stiff. Be cool. Graceful." She jumped in front of him. "You know what?"

"What?"

"Here's how to think of it. Your walk should

65

talk. It should say, Hey, world, watch out, here I come. I know where I'm going and nothing's going to stop me. That doesn't mean I'm a brute. I'm not. I'm actually very sensitive and caring, not to mention romantic. It's just that I'm confident. I know how to succeed. If you're smart, you'll keep your eyes on me."

Eddie whistled. "That's a lot for one walk to say."

"Pooh," said Salem. "Just do it." She snapped her fingers, fluttered her hand. "Go on, walk."

Eddie walked, or tried to. Suddenly, it seemed so complicated. Head, shoulders, step, cool, graceful, sensitive, romantic, confident. He felt like all sticks and rubber bands. He barely made it to the other side of the room. He almost felt out of breath. It used to be so easy.

"Not bad," said Salem, surprising him. "With a little practice, who knows. Now this time I want you to put a little swagger into it. Take charge. It's like you're the only pro walker around here, the rest of us clods are amateurs. Come on, swagger."

He swaggered.

She laughed. "Whoa! Not that much. Cut back a little."

He cut back on the swagger. According to her directions, he turned up the sensitive, shortened his step, lengthened his step, projected his confidence, back and forth across the room, five, ten, fifteen times.

Salem pulled down her window shades, turned out the overhead light, and draped a red sweater over her desk lamp. "That's as close as I can get to making it like a dance. Okay — here I am, Sunny Wyler, standing in the corner with Salem Brownmiller, watching the action, when who comes *walking* by — "

Eddie came walking. Salem nodded. "Yeah, not bad. Now we have to work on the rest."

"What rest?"

"Clothes."

He squealed. "I can't go buying all new clothes." He glanced at Salem's digital clock. "And I gotta be home for dinner in ten minutes." He started backing toward the door.

Salem thought fast, talked fast. "Okay . . . okay. Listen. You don't need all new clothes. You just need something different. To be noticed. Something that makes a statement. Something that says — "

"Oh, great," said Eddie, "now my clothes have to talk, too."

"Shhh!" Salem silenced him. She closed her eyes, balled her fists, clutched her writing scarf. "Think . . . *think* . . ." Her eyes shot open. "I got it!" She squeezed his arm — "Wait here" — and fled the room. She returned with something that, to Eddie, looked like a giant three-foot-long Slim Jim beef stick.

"What is *that?*"

Salem tapped it once upon the floor. "A cane. It used to be my grandfather's. He called it a swizzle stick."

"I don't need a cane," said Eddie. "There's nothing wrong with my leg."

Salem laughed. "It's not for walking, goofy. It's for style. You just carry it."

This time it was Eddie who laughed. "You gotta be kidding."

"I'm perfectly serious," she said, looking perfectly serious. "You want to be noticed, don't you?"

"Not *that* noticed."

"Oh, you conformists. Here." She thrust the cane at him until he took hold of it. "It'll work, you'll see."

"Okay," said Eddie, hurrying from the room before she came up with anything else. Halfway down the stairs he was halted by her call. "Eddie!"

He turned. "What?"

"I almost forgot. This is really important."

"Salem, I'm late."

"Don't speak to her."

"*Huh?*"

"Don't speak to her. At the dance. When you come walking, just walk on by. Don't say anything." She came down one step. "Even *more* important. Don't even *look* at her. Pretend she's not there."

"That's crazy."

"Trust me."

"What if she talks to me?"

"Pretend you don't hear. Pretend you have more important things to do."

Eddie was backing down the stairs. "What if she asks me a question? Right to my face."

"Say — " Salem thought a moment, took another step down. "Say, 'Later, babe.' Whatever she says, you say that, and walk away."

"Later, babe?"

"Right."

By now Salem was halfway down the stairs. Eddie was at the door. He felt for the knob, opened the door, stepped outside.

"And walk away!"

He shut the door. Her last words came through: "And twirl the cane!"

After dinner, on the telephone with Pickles, Eddie told of his session with Salem.

"Come on over," said Pickles. "I'll show you the only move you'll ever need."

14

It was supposed to be a dance, but maybe they should have called it a war. As Pickles and Eddie approached the school on Friday evening, squads of kids, mostly eighth-graders, were stalking and marching and darting this way and that, calling up the alleys, huddling in dark knots.

"Fights tonight," said Pickles.

Eddie nodded. "At the dance?"

"Maybe. Probably after."

"Think we'll see any?"

"Could be."

Salem was right about one thing: There were a lot of fights. But they were hardly the gory massacres that Salem made them out to be. Often they never got past the yelling and threatening stage. If there was action, it often as not began and ended with pushing, accompanied by the word *yeah*, as in:

"Yeah?"

"Yeah."

"Yeah?"

"Yeah!"

Once in a while, the pushing became grabbing, and the grabbing became yanking, and the yanking became wrestling. Then you'd have the two warriors grappling and hugging and grunting, at which point the war did in fact begin to resemble a dance. Hopefully, from the other kids' point of view, they would topple to the ground and roll around there for a while. But even this was usually disappointing, since the best thing that happened was that the "fighters" had their shirts pulled up over their heads.

No, when you got right down to it, a fight was not really a fight until a punch was thrown. And the fact was, that rarely happened. Yet the possibility that it might happen was precisely what drew the crowds when someone shouted, "Fight!"

Eddie was no exception. He felt the excitement, the thrill. He would claw his way to the front of the mob to see a fist land on a nose. Did that mean he was a barbarian, as Salem might say? A savage? If he were living in ancient Rome, at the Colosseum watching two gladiators battle to the death, would he be up in the stands cheering and yelling with the rest of them and giving the thumbs-down sign?

Eddie didn't know. He didn't think that deeply about it. All he knew was that he liked to watch a fight, and so did a lot of other kids, and he didn't know how to explain it to Salem. It was just there.

He did know one thing, though. When Angelpuss butted his nose in gym class, he had been as terrified of being the center of attention as of her. He knew now more than ever that there was only one way he would ever be involved in a fight: as a spectator.

The dance was in the cafeteria, though Eddie hardly recognized it. The tables were gone and most of the chairs. What was left was a huge square room. Music poured out of the dark onto a bare linoleum flatness as big as a prairie. People, hordes of them, swarmed around the edges.

Eddie nodded toward the bare expanse in the middle. "That where you're supposed to dance?"

"Yep," said Pickles.

"Nobody's there."

"They will be. When things warm up." Pickles gave him a knowing wink and a grin.

Eddie kind of hoped they never would warm up. In fact, along about now he kind of wished he had just stayed at home, spent a nice, safe night in front of the TV. He had not brought the cane, nor was he walking as he had practiced at Salem's. He was nothing more or less than the usual Eddie Mott.

"I don't know about this," he said.

"You don't have to know," said Pickles. "Just do it."

"I'm nervous."

Pickles fanned him with his hand. "Don't sweat. It's a piece a cake."

"How do we know it'll work?"

"Trust me."

"That's what Salem said."

"It's guaranteed. Girls can't resist."

Eddie scanned the mob. "Think she's here yet?"

Pickles looked. "Don't know. Hard to tell. There's plenty of time."

Kids were still streaming through the door. The noise was beginning to top the music. Eighth-graders, raucous as crows in treetops, called to one another across the room.

Pickles tugged Eddie's sleeve. "Come on."

"Where?"

"There."

Pickles was pointing to the other side of the cafeteria.

"Okay," said Eddie. He started around the perimeter.

"No," said Pickles, "this way." He pulled Eddie into the great open space.

Eddie dug in his heels. "Hold it! Not that way."

Pickles said, "Come on, I think I see her over there," and yanked Eddie along with him.

Eddie felt as exposed as a bug crawling across

a white porcelain sink. Any instant he expected to be flattened by a swatter. He could barely believe it when they reached the other side. He looked around. "I don't see her."

Pickles grinned. "I lied. Just getting you ready for the spotlight."

Suddenly Eddie was bumped sideways, and someone said, "Oh, excuse me."

It was a nickelhead.

"Oh, excuse me," came another voice, from another nickelhead, whose shoulder sent Eddie staggering into yet another bump. "Oh, excuse *me*."

The third bump sent him reeling into a girl, a nickelchick, Angelpuss. "Well, well," she beamed, "we meet again." She gave his cheek a tweak, and then he was gone, swept away by Pickles.

They didn't stop till they reached the refreshment table. Eddie was flushed and panting, his nose twitching like a rabbit's. "I could've died."

"I wouldn't have let you," said Pickles. "Have a soda. I'm buying." Pickles laid money down and took two sodas and a bag of pretzels. He pulled out a pretzel and practically stuffed it into Eddie's mouth. "Eat. Help you get back to normal."

Eddie was munching and sipping and trying to calm down when Pickles said, "There they are."

Eddie looked. Sunny and Salem were heading their way. Eddie almost choked.

Pickles slipped behind him and whispered, "Okay, you know the plan."

"I can't." Eddie said the words without moving his lips.

Pickles poked him in the back and sent him forward. "Go."

The plan called for Eddie to avoid Sunny until he made his move. In the meantime, Pickles would take care of business.

Propelled by Pickles' push, Eddie moved ahead, straight toward Sunny and Salem. Eddie knew that Salem must be wondering where the cane and walk were. He saw them slow down. And suddenly, brilliantly, he found a way to follow both Pickles' and Salem's advice. He walked right on past them — he could feel their astonished eyes — but not before muttering, kind of low and out of the side of his mouth, "Later, babe."

Oh, how he wished, as he blended into the crowd, that he could turn and see the look on Sunny's face!

15

As the girls approached Pickles, Salem was stifling a grin and Sunny was saying, tossing a thumb back in Eddie's general direction, "I think he's finally gone cuckoo."

"Nah," said Pickles nonchalantly, "he's just scouting around."

"Scouting?" said Sunny. "What for?"

Pickles chuckled. He gestured at the crowd. "What else? Girls."

Sunny's snorty laugh was so sudden and forceful that she had to quick blow her nose. "Yeah, right," she snickered. "Romeo Mott."

Pickles shrugged. "Believe it or not."

"I'll not," said Sunny and ordered a soda.

First to start dancing were a half dozen nickelcouples. Within seconds the perimeter flooded inward, and the empty space in the middle vanished for the night.

After finishing her soda plus a bag of pretzels

and a bag of popcorn, Sunny stood for a full minute watching the action. Then she said, "Okay, what now?"

The same question had occurred to Salem. Her whole focus had been to drag Sunny to the dance, partly for Eddie, partly as company for herself. Now Sunny was here, Eddie was gone, and so was Pickles. "Where do you think the guys disappeared to?" she asked, stalling for time.

"I don't know," said Sunny, "but I'm gonna disappear in a minute if somebody doesn't tell me what I'm doing here."

"It's a dance," said Salem. "Want to dance?"

Sunny answered with a long and dirty look.

Secretly Salem herself wished someone would tell her what she was doing here. Though she acted like a veteran of these things, the fact was this was her first dance ever.

Until now, when the word *dance* was mentioned, the first thing that came to Salem's mind was the championship ballroom dancing that she watched every year on the public television station. She imagined herself swirling in a pastel gown in the arms of a dashing man in a tuxedo. She loved the grace and elegance and romance of it all.

Tonight, looking over the cafeteria dance floor, she found neither grace nor elegance. As for romance, well, if there was any out there, it sure wasn't aimed in her direction. Still, she could not help wondering if even now, right here, Cupid was drawing back his bowstring. Was someone watching? Someone fated to enter her life tomorrow, next week, next year? Perhaps to cleverly bump into her around a corner, or to wisely need to borrow a quarter from her in a lunch line. Watching her even now as she stood by the refreshment table sipping soda. The thought of it made her stop swallowing, raise her chin, and produce a faint, alluring smile.

"I don't believe it," said Sunny.

Salem broke from her cobweb of reverie. "Huh?"

"Look."

In the middle of the floor Mr. Brimlow, Plumstead's bow-tied principal, was doing a moonwalk that resembled a backward stumble through a pothole patch. And then he was out of sight, enclosed by a mob of clapping, whistling students.

"Aren't you glad you came now?" asked Salem.

Sunny did not answer, which meant, for the time being at least, yes.

The two girls spent the next hour looking: Sunny for something as entertaining as Mr. Brimlow's pothole walk, Salem for somebody looking at her. Before long, Salem had convinced herself that half the boys in the place were eyeing her. She could feel them checking her out, this sixth-grade girl with the long brown hair and long skirt. Ah, but they were sneaky, those boys, always turning away just before she looked their way, pretending to be looking elsewhere, talking to their friends. She began swaying a tiny bit to the music, bobbing her head to the beat, to show she was available in case any of them worked up the nerve to ask her to dance.

Meanwhile, Sunny consumed three more sodas, two bags of popcorn, a bag of pizza-flavored nachos, and three full-sized Kit Kat bars. When the next mob of clappers and whistlers converged on the dance floor, Sunny pulled Salem away from the sideline. "Sounds like Brim's at it again. Let's get a good view this time."

Both girls were fond of Mr. Brimlow. Along with Pickles and Eddie, they comprised his so-called Principal's Posse, four sixth-graders that he had lunch with once a week. The mob was even bigger and louder this time, totally obscuring the center of attention. They were going wild.

"Maybe he's taking off his bow tie," quipped Sunny.

It was hopeless trying to see over the heads of the cheering mob, many of whom were taller seventh- and eighth-graders. So the girls wormed and squirmed their way between bodies until they found themselves right behind the front row. Neither of them, not if they had traded eyeballs, could believe what they saw.

16

It was Eddie and Pickles.

Dancing.

Even Eddie couldn't believe it.

He had spent the last hour blending in with the crowd, visiting the boys' room, hiding. He knew Pickles would be coming for him, to carry out the plan. But he just couldn't get up the nerve to do it.

The thing was, this was so unlike anything he had ever done before. He had tried to make Pickles understand that the other night, but all Pickles would do was shrug and say, "So? First time for everything."

Lurking from shadow to shadow, Eddie had come to understand what the terms *clammy* and *cold feet* meant.

Of course, Pickles finally found him. "Let's go. Where've you been?"

"Right here. Where've *you* been?"

Pickles scowled. "Forget it. Next song we do it."

The chill from Eddie's feet was rising. He now had cold ankles, shins, and knees. "I don't know."

"You don't need to know. Just do it."

Pickles was casually looking over the dance floor, bobbing his head to the music. Eddie couldn't get over how easy Pickles was about everything, how fearless.

"I don't think I'm ready."

"You're ready," said Pickles, bobbing. "That's why we practiced. You're ready."

"I stink."

Pickles turned, poked him in the chest. "You don't stink. I taught you everything you know. You can't stink."

The music ended. Some dancers headed for the sidelines, some hung where they were, awaiting the next record. Eddie's ears were cold. Next thing he knew, he was out in the middle of the floor, dancing.

It was Pickles' invention. He had taught it to Eddie, and they had practiced it over and over yesterday after school and after dinner. It was all based on skateboarding. The basic step was to keep your left foot still while you paddled with the right, then slide the left ahead, then paddle with the right some more: paddle, slide, paddle, slide. Like driving a skateboard along a sidewalk.

There were all kinds of moves you could make off that: curb jumps, whirlies, high-bank turns. You could even keep both feet still, spread just right, hold your arms out wide, and sort of teeter and sway as though you were zinging down a monster hill at sixty per.

Any other time you were free to do pretty much what you wanted with your arms. Pickles liked to throw one arm straight out ahead and the other behind, making him look like a cross-country skier. Eddie liked to bend his arms halfway, make fists, and do a circular, chugging motion.

The tip of Eddie's tongue was firmly in the grip of his teeth as he concentrated on the music and his own feet. Pickles meanwhile was free-lancing all over the place, improvising moves as he went along. Eddie stayed with the basics: paddle, slide, paddle, slide. He did try a whirlie once and surprised himself that it went so well. His first clue that Pickles had been right came about twenty seconds into the record, when a nearby voice called, "Hey, check this out!"

Pickles heard it, too. Halfway through a U-turn, he flashed Eddie a wink and a grin.

Eddie became aware of motion around him subsiding: Dancers were stopping to watch. And now they were coming, rushing even, from all directions, surrounding them, totally engulfing them, like he had seen them do to Mr. Brimlow earlier on.

Somebody whistled, somebody called "Do it!", somebody clapped. and from then on the mob lent its own percussion and lyrics to the music.

"It's the Pickles kid!"

"Who's the other one?"

"They're only sixth-graders!"

"They're doin' it!"

"Go!"

"Yeah!"

Someone leaned in, cupped his hands, and yelled, "What's it called?"

Pickles whirled twice and shot back, "Funky pickle!"

There was a second of stillness while the mob digested this, then they exploded, cheering, whistling, stomping the floor while shouts of "Funky pickle!" and "Awesome!" filled the night.

Eddie kept expecting to wake up from a dream. But until he did, he had to admit Pickles was right. It was turning out just as he had said. Now there was only one thing left to fall into place.

Was she out there, in that dark, stomping, cheering crowd? Was she watching him, seeing him in a new light, thinking *Hey, that's not the Eddie Mott I know*, feeling something?

Oh, she was, all right. She was out there, among the dark faces, watching, feeling. Only one difference: She wasn't the she that Eddie had in mind.

Not even close.

17

Monday morning in the hallways.
Half the student body, it seemed, was funky pickling down the corridors of Plumstead. Paddle, slide, paddle, slide, *twirl*. Pickles and Eddie couldn't show their faces without somebody calling:

"Hey!"

"Yo!"

"Pickle dudes!"

"Check it!"

Pickles grinned slightly. "Like the dance never ended."

Eddie gushed. "We're famous!"

But he wondered how famous he was with a certain person. Eddie never did see Sunny for the rest of the dance. He and Pickles spent the night putting on exhibitions and teaching the others how to do it. As a matter of fact, Eddie had not laid eyes on Sunny all weekend, and now, as praise rained down upon him in the hallways, he ached to end the suspense.

He cornered Salem in English. "Did she see? Was she watching? Did she say anything? What do you think?"

Salem flinched under the barrage. "Calm *down.*"

He calmed down and repeated the questions.

Salem opened her grammar book and sighed. "Yes, she saw you. No, she didn't say anything. And what I think is that I don't have any more time to spare for you and your love life. The stories for the Willow Wembley contest are due this week, and that's the only thing I'm giving my attention to. I must *not* be distracted. I worked on my story all weekend. I eat, sleep, and think my story twenty-four hours a day, and until it's finished you and the rest of the world are *persona non grata.*" She turned from Eddie and stared straight ahead as Miss Comstock began the class.

Well, whatever *persona non grata* meant, the nail-biting fact was that next period was math, and Sunny was in the class. As Miss Comstock read from a Willow Wembley novel, Eddie stewed in his questions. How would Sunny act? Would she compliment him on his dancing? Say she was sorry she had turned down his invitation? Would she write him a note? *Did* she write him a note? He riffled through his books, turned them page-end down, shook them. No, there was no note.

Most important of all, would there be a different look to her face? The look that he had seen other girls give other guys. The look that said, *I like you.*

In short: no. None of it happened. When Eddie saw her in math, she was no more or less than the usual Sunny. He tried to convince himself that her eye had a twinkle that hadn't been there before, that her lips curled in a way that meant something. But when, at the end of class, Sunny popped out of her seat and, without so much as glancing at him, flipped her hand and said, "Later, 'gator," well, Eddie knew that Pickles for once in his life had been wrong.

He was still feeling down when lunchtime came around. Instead of seeking out his friends as usual, he walked down the lunch line by himself. He wasn't very hungry, and he didn't feel like being healthy. He picked out a package of peanut butter crackers and a chocolate milk. He was reaching for a bag of potato chips when a voice behind him, female and as friendly as could be, said, "Hi, Eddie."

He turned. Orange hair spike. Purple lipstick. Angelpuss.

She looked at his tray. "Not hungry today?"

"Guess not," Eddie replied. He felt blindly for the potato chips. He was afraid if he took his eyes off her, she would butt him in the nose. He felt very tense being this close to her. He put all his systems on red alert, ready to jump aside if that forehead came darting forward. His nose itched and ached. The spike made her a six-footer.

She reached into the potato chip bin and pulled out two packs. She smiled. "Want one?" Eddie shrugged, half nodded. She put a pack on his tray. "Maybe I'll be a waitress someday," she giggled. Her nose ring gleamed like a tiny, misplaced halo.

Eddie peeked at the line behind her. He didn't see Weasel.

"That was some dance you guys did the other night," she said.

Eddie edged toward the cashier, trying to put some distance between himself and the girl. "Thanks."

She closed the gap. He moved farther. She closed the gap. She stayed close, smiling her purple smile. The leading edge of her tray was smack against the trailing edge of his. "Oh, look!" she squealed, way too loud. "Our trays are kissing!"

Eddie's face boiled. He was sure he must look to all the world like Tommy Tomato. He rammed his tray up to the cashier, paid his money, and headed for the tables. He found an empty one in the corner. He sat down — and so did she, taking the seat to his right.

"Boy," she said, opening a carton of juice, "I'm hungry as a hog." A pair of chili dogs lay on her plate. She picked one up and devoured half of it in one bite. She chewed for a full minute, closing her eyes and going, "Mmm . . . mmm . . ."

"Just think," she said, "it was right here where it started. What's it called, the dance?"

"Funky pickle," Eddie replied. For the first time, the name felt silly on his lips.

"That's it, yeah!" She rapped a fork on the table. "Funky pickle." Then, while Eddie watched helplessly, she jumped up from her seat and did a few funky picklesteps.

Kids at nearby tables applauded. Angelpuss took a bow and sat down. Eddie was mortified. The whole lunchroom was staring at his table. The only good news was that he didn't see Weasel, or any other nickelhead for that matter.

Eddie worked on his potato chips and peanut butter crackers, just to keep busy. He prayed she would go away, but instead she settled back, finished off her first chili dog, and said, "So, you got a girlfriend?"

What kind of a question is that? Eddie wondered. "No," he said, "guess not."

She smiled enormously. "Good."

Now what did she mean by *that*?

Next thing Eddie knew, her hand was coming at him. A punch? He flinched back, but she leaned, and her hand kept coming till it landed on his nose, softly. Her fingertips patted it. His eyeballs moved around his sockets like slugs in a pinball machine.

"Sorry I butted you," she said. Her voice was

full of sympathy. And her face — Eddie couldn't believe it — had the look he had been hoping to find on Sunny. "Maybe I should kiss it to make it feel better." She was coming closer: the face, the orange spike, the purple lips.

Eddie recoiled with such force that both he and his chair toppled backward onto the floor. The place exploded in laughter. The bell rang, adding its own ridicule. Eddie left all as it was — the chair, the lunch, the girl — and sprinted for the safety of the hallway.

18

Eddie had been dreading it, and sure enough it happened. He was walking innocently down the hall to his last class when suddenly he was walking on air. Hands had grabbed the shoulders of his shirt, lifted, and now he was floating down the hall like Peter Pan, except Peter Pan was never hung between two nickelheads. And they were two of the biggest of all, pure giants.

"In there," came a familiar voice from behind.

As he continued to skim over the floor, Eddie wrenched his neck to look. It was Weasel. He sailed through a boys' room door. "There," said Weasel, and Eddie was deposited on top of a sink. His feet dangled in air. His mind flashed back to a high chair, himself in it. But this was not home, and the face before him was not his mother's.

Weasel had a sharp, triangular face. His haircut could not fit as many polka-dot bare spots as other nickelheads because his nickelhead was on the small side. He was rolling a jawbreaker around in his mouth. It was making his tongue green. "What's this about you and my chick?" His sugary jawbreaker breath poured the words into Eddie's face.

"Wh — " Eddie tried to speak, but all that came out was a gravelly croak. He tried again. "Wha — " Getting better. The third time he nailed it. "What do you mean?"

"I mean at lunch. I mean sitting with my chick. I mean trying to lay lips on my chick."

Eddie gasped. "Who?"

"You." As punctuation, Weasel poked Eddie until he was sitting in the bowl of the sink. It happened to be a perfect fit.

The best Eddie could do was babble: "Me . . . huh . . . no . . . who . . . her . . . huh . . ."

Weasel placed the tip of his index finger between Eddie's eyes. "You go near her again, you're dead meat." He pushed Eddie's head as he backed away. Eddie's backward motion carried him into the cold water knob, which turned just enough to bring water from the faucet. Eddie leapt from the sink — too late — the seat of his pants was soaked. The three nickelheads went out the door in stitches.

Eddie tried fanning his fanny with his hand to dry his pants. He tried blotting them dry with paper towels. Realizing then that only time would dry him, he remained in the boys' room. He did not go to his last class. He did not go to homeroom.

He did not sneak out of the building until 4:30 that afternoon.

After dinner Eddie phoned Pickles and told him what happened. "He said I was dead meat."

"Don't worry," said Pickles. "He's not going to kill you. Maybe beat-up meat, that's all."

Eddie shrieked. "Oh, great!"

Pickles chuckled into the receiver. "Just kidding. Hey, I told you that dance was powerful stuff, didn't I?"

"Yeah?" Eddie retorted bitterly. "Well, it didn't do nothing to the one it was *supposed* to do something to."

"Maybe she just won't admit it."

"Maybe I'm dead meat."

"Hey, get off that. He was just trying to scare you."

"Trying? He did."

"Listen, if you're worried, all you have to do is stay away from her. And anyway, she was probably just joking around. You probably saw the last of her."

Eddie wished.

Next morning, on the way to get his books, there she was, waiting at his locker. He did a quick U-turn, ran up the steps, along the hall, down another stairway, and darted into homeroom from the other side. In every class that morning he got into trouble because he didn't have his book.

At lunch he hooked up with Pickles, figured he was safe. She wasn't in sight. Halfway through the line he heard, "Hi, Eddie." He bolted, leaving Pickles with two trays. He spent lunch period in the darkness of the music room's instrument closet, aching for tacos and burgers among the trombones and clarinets.

After school, sure enough, she was at his locker. He ran straight home.

"I couldn't go to my locker all day," he complained to Pickles over the phone. "I didn't have any books. I didn't eat lunch. I'm a wreck."

"What can I say?" said Pickles. "You're irresistible to the opposite sex."

"Funny. And two times I passed Weasel in the halls. He gave me this look, I can't even describe it. And you know what else?"

"What else?"

"He makes his hand like a gun, with his finger out, you know?"

"Yeah?"

"And he, like, aims with one eye shut and goes, 'Pow.' "

"So? He's playing cops and robbers."

"And I didn't even tell you the worst thing yet."

"Tell me."

Eddie paused. He lowered his voice. "I'm being watched."

Pickles suppressed a chuckle. "Yeah? By who?"

"The nickelheads, who do you think? I can feel their eyes on me. Everywhere I go. I'm afraid even to go to the bathroom. If they ever catch me in there again . . ." Eddie left the unspeakable thought unspoken.

"No sweat," said Pickles. "Just make sure you go to the bathroom before you leave the house in the morning, and don't drink water all day."

Eddie didn't answer, unsure if Pickles was kidding or not.

"And anyway," Pickles added, "things will probably cool off tomorrow."

Eddie groaned into the phone. "No *way*! That's the *really* worst thing of all."

"It is?"

"Yeah. Tomorrow I have gym class, and Angelpuss and Weasel are both in it."

19

Salem had her own problems, number one being how to keep the rest of the world away while you're trying to write the story that will determine the success or failure of the rest of your life.

In recent days Salem's future had begun to show itself. It looked something like this: Salem wins Willow Wembley contest. Along with seventh- and eighth-grade winners, Salem escorts the great author around the school on Willow Wembley Day. Miss Wembley is dazzled by Salem's knowledge and vocabulary and maturity and refinement and elegance and all-around *savoir faire*. In fact, they even speak a little French to each other.

But most of all, Willow Wembley is impressed with Salem's story. She asks to see more of Salem's work, which Salem pulls out of her book bag (having cleverly anticipated such a request). Once Miss Wembley begins reading, she cannot stop. She drags Salem into a vacant room and reads and reads. Her eyes bulge in wonder. She wags her head and says things like, "This is incredible!" and "Are you sure you didn't copy this?" and "Are you sure you're only in sixth grade?"

Then she rushes to a telephone and calls her publisher and says, "I have just discovered the next great writer of our time. Send her a contract." And Salem signs a contract and writes a five-hundred-page book, and it's a smash, it's bigger than *Gone With the Wind*, it's made into a movie, and Salem writes the screenplay and swoops onto the stage in Hollywood to accept the Academy Award . . .

Or something like that.

Wrapping her writing scarf about her, Salem experienced the week as if in a cocoon. Home, school, day, night — all was a gray, muffled blur beyond the fierce concentration with which she bore down on her story.

Every minute away from her Left Bank garret was a minute lost. Only there, with the door closed and the Eiffel Tower looking down, did her artistic soul feel at home. From handwritten notes to computer keyboard to laser printer, she wrote and rewrote, corrected and deleted and added and clarified and simplified and polished and repolished until, at precisely 9:46 Thursday evening, the last page of the second correction of the ninth improvement of the third version came sliding from her father's Hewlett Packard LaserJet.

The relief, the exhilaration, the occasion of it brought tears to her eyes. Ten pages. Two thousand one hundred and thirty words. So light to hold, nearly weightless, and most of that was paper. Take away the paper, she fancied, and the LaserJetted letters, the powdery, unmoored words would probably rise like thistledown against gravity, hang forever in the cosmos. Ten little pages: one future, her world to be.

Salem keyboarded and printed out a title page. She drilled tidy holes in the pages with her three-hole punch. She inserted and fastened them in a sky blue, fresh-from-the-drugstore binder.

She took off her writing scarf and draped it over the back of her chair. She turned out the light. She toppled into her bed like a felled tree. Forget brushing, forget pajamas. But exhausted as she was, she could not sleep. Though she had dismounted, the steed that had borne her still raced on, mane flying, foaming at the bit. She turned on her twelve-inch TV, kept the volume at a whisper, and saw shows at hours she had barely known to exist.

Next morning she handed her story to Miss Comstock.

Coming out of class, she gave Eddie a playful shoulder bump. "Good morning, Mister Mott."

Eddie looked at her like something he found between his toes.

"What's the matter?" she inquired cheerily.

"What's the matter?" he squawked. "What's the *matter*? Now you ask. I'm a dead man, I'm a slab a salami, *that's* what's the matter. I'll never see twelve. I'll never be a teenager. I'll never drive a car. I don't even know what I'm doing in school. I might as well go straight to the cemetery and start digging my own grave." His eyes were flashing, his nostrils flaring. "Yeah, that's where I'll go. You got a shovel? Anybody got a shovel?"

Salem had seen him like this before. He tended to go overboard when upset, not unlike herself. She touched him gently on the arm. She looked into his wild eyes. "Hey — hey — it's me. Salem. Calm down. Tell me what happened."

He calmed down and told her. He told her about the day in gym class. About Angelpuss chasing him all over the field and grabbing him and pulling out his red tail and tying it around her neck and strutting around yapping, "Eddie Mott loves me!"

"What did that Weasel creature do?"

"He wasn't there. He was absent that day."

"So what happened then?"

Eddie fished a piece of paper from his pocket, uncrumpled it. "This." There were two words in black marker:

DEAD MEAT

Above the words was a tiny hole in the paper.

"This was tacked to my front door when I left for school next day. His spies must have told him about it. Good thing my parents didn't see it."

Salem cringed just to look at it. "Why didn't you tell me about this before?"

Eddie's eyes bulged. "*Tell* you? What do you think I've been *trying* to do?"

The bell rang. Eddie ran for his class, leaving Salem with the paper. She could not take her eyes from it, this evidence from the violent world around her. It seemed to grow hot and burn evilly in her fingers. She tossed it to the floor and rushed for class.

Later that day Salem was talking with Pickles.

"So what is it with this Angelpuss creature anyway? Why is she being this way with Eddie?"

Pickles shrugged. "Love, I guess."

Salem scoffed, "Oh, right, sure. She's in eighth grade, he's in sixth. Not to mention that Eddie looks like he only belongs in fourth or fifth. And double not to mention that she's one of these nickelcreatures. I thought they all stick together."

Another shrug from Pickles. "Love conquers all."

"I'm going to kick you if you don't get serious."

"Kick? I thought you were against violence."
Salem folded her arms and glared in silence. "All I know," said Pickles, "is what she tells Eddie."

"Which is?"

"Which is, she has the hots for him."

"Hots? You've got to be kidding."

"That's the word."

Salem stared, blinking. "Why?"

"I guess it started with the funky pickle. She says ever since she saw him doing it at the dance, she can't stop thinking about him."

"And Eddie, what about him?"

"He tries to stay away from her, but she catches up to him once or twice a day."

"And the Weasel creature?"

"He put a note on Eddie's front door."

"He showed me."

Pickles looked surprised. "Well . . ."

They fell silent for a while.

"So," Salem resumed, "what now?"

Pickles shrugged. "Fight, I guess."

Salem stomped her foot. "Oh, really. Fight. Like that's the answer to everything. Little Eddie? That's the most ridiculous thing I ever heard in my life."

"Tell that to Weasel."

Salem marched off, marched back. She shook her head, still trying to make sense of it all. "I thought this Angelpuss was supposed to be this Weasel's girlfriend."

"She was."

"And now she doesn't like him anymore? She

likes Eddie Mott? Our Eddie Mott?"

"Looks that way."

Salem paced some more. "Okay, so, if it's true, ridiculous as it sounds, the girl actually likes Eddie, why doesn't this Weasel character go find himself another girlfriend?"

"You'll have to ask him. All I know is, Eddie's scared stiff. He's been, for a couple of days now." He said this looking straight into Salem's eyes.

Salem blinked. "You're mad at me."

"I didn't say that."

"But you are, aren't you?" Pickles looked away. "You're mad because I wasn't paying attention to all this, because I was busy writing my story."

"So were we."

"It was just an assignment for you."

He said nothing.

"Pickles, that story is the most important thing in the world to me. My whole future could depend on it."

Pickles nodded, hands in pockets.

"Ohhh!" Salem stomped. Many feelings bubbled inside her, but only guilt boiled over. It oozed across every bright meadow of her being until she felt as rank and lifeless as lettuce in a gutter, as vile as a virus. It was not only an unwelcome feeling, it was most untimely; for on the eve of her greatest triumph, there was simply no room in her life for a rotten intruder. And so she got rid of it, expelled it, replaced it with a feeling of her own making, an old familiar feeling.

"Well," she sniffed primly, turning to Pickles, "I tried to stop you all from being savages. This is what happens when you live by the sword. It serves him right."

And off she marched.

20

On Monday Eddie found another note tacked to his front door. It said:

FRIDAY AFTER SCHOOL

"I have five days to live," he told Pickles as they raised the flag at school that morning.

Pickles finished playing reveille on his battered and ancient bugle. He put his arm around Eddie's shoulders. He smiled. "Don't worry."

Don't worry?

How could Eddie not worry? Tell that to his hand, which sweated so much all day that it practically shrunk his pencil. Tell that to his nose, which twitched from first period till last.

Following Pickles' advice, he avoided drinking fountains and lavatories. Nevertheless, in spite of consuming nothing more liquid than honey-lemon cough drops, he barely made it home in time to go to the bathroom, after which he guzzled down two glasses of cranapple juice and a can of cherry cola.

Salem stayed after school. She joined several other volunteers, under the direction of Miss Comstock, in creating a Willow Wembley display in the glass case in the lobby. It featured copies of the author's books along with artifacts of her most famous characters, the Klatterfields: a wooden pipe, such as Clyde Klatterfield continually smoked while taming a spot in the wilderness for his family; a pressed dandelion, such as thirteen-year-old Tara Klatterfield might have created; and a teacup and saucer, for even in the wilderness, never did the Klatterfields fail to have high tea at four o'clock by the homemade sundial.

And, of course, there was a photograph of Willow Wembley herself. It was bigger and better than any of her dust jacket photos. The great author was shown in profile, gazing out over a harbor from a dramatically high promontory. Her skirt was full and long, like Salem's; her sleeves were flouncy. She was the very portrait of elegance, the crowning jewel of humankind's long and fitful reach for perfection.

To think that in four days Salem would be in Willow Wembley's presence was almost too much to bear. She caught herself daydreaming numerous times throughout the day. This was no problem in class, but when, on the way home from school, she awoke to the squeal of brakes and discovered herself inches from a car bumper in the middle of a street, that was something else. She literally slapped herself for almost committing the most unspeakable blunder of all time: getting herself killed before Friday.

That evening Eddie Mott, instead of doing homework, wrote out his will.

21

Tuesday morning Eddie awoke to a golden glow. It was the window shades. He had awakened in this room approximately four thousand times in his life, yet never, until now, had he noticed how the dull pale of the shades became magically transformed by the morning sun behind them. He lingered in bed, he smiled, he bathed in the warm, butterscotch blessing.

Vanished were the frightful hours of the night, when he had been visited by memories of the time he came closest to a fight. He was in fourth grade, innocently playing basketball on a dusty park playground, when a burly kid he didn't know started pushing him and pushing till he'd slammed back into a chain link fence. As the kid reached out, Eddie ran, ran like he had never run before, ran till there was nothing but clear pavement and the echoes of his own footsteps behind him. He was safe. He headed for home. He cried. He didn't want to, but the tears just came. And for the first time he saw, and had seen ever since, that he was a coward.

For two years he had secretly hated this about himself. He had seen other kids go swinging into battle with one another. He marveled at their zest for combat and cursed himself for having none. His way was to make a smile, not a fist. While he thrilled to the brawl of others, for himself he relished peace. He asked only to be safe and unafraid.

And now his worst nightmare had come true. The call that used to bring him running — "Fight!" — now chilled his bones. In three days he would be standing somewhere outside Plumstead Middle School, maybe on a patch of grass, maybe on a blacktopped parking lot or driveway. Across from him would be Weasel Munshak. Surrounding the two of them would be a ring of spectators, kids, hundreds of them. Classmates who had sat beside him minutes before would now be yelling for his blood. Weasel would move closer, and the only question, the most terrible question in all the world was: Would he start to cry after he got hit in the face, or before?

In any case, Eddie figured that by five o'clock Friday afternoon, as the rest of the town was quitting work and heading home to their families, he would be a croaker on a cement slab.

In the golden glow of the window shades, it all seemed a bad dream. Even his will on the dresser seemed like some leftover from a game he must have played. He read the opening words — "I, Edward Albert Mott, do leave behind to my parents . . ." — and chuckled and tossed the paper aside.

Forty minutes later, as he stepped outside to find a note tacked to the front door:

THREE DAYS

he knew again that it was no dream.

In English class, Salem avoided Eddie's eyes and locked into Miss Comstock's. She had handed in her story on Friday morning. It was now Tuesday morning. The judges — three English teachers, one of them Miss Comstock — must surely have read all the entries by now. Were they still making up their minds? Had they narrowed it down to five or ten finalists from each grade? Had they already decided? Were the winners' names in a sealed envelope somewhere?

Miss Comstock read two chapters from *The Owl Hoo Came to Dinner*. She was pacing the reading in order to finish on Thursday, the day before Willow Wembley's arrival. Salem searched her eyes, her face, her body language for clues. No fewer than four times did the teacher's eyes come up from the book to meet Salem's. Twice her lips seemed to hold a faint smile. Was Miss Comstock sending a signal? Was the faint smile saying, "Yes,

Salem, you did it. I knew you would"?

When class ended, Salem lingered at her desk, pretending to rearrange her books. Within seconds the two of them were alone in the room.

Salem kept her eyes down. She took her breath in silent sips. She was aware of Miss Comstock fussing at her desk. Any moment she expected to hear: "Salem, now that we're alone . . ."

It didn't happen. When Salem finally dared to look up, Miss Comstock was breezing out of the room with a briefcase and a cheery, "See you tomorrow, Salem."

Maddening!

When the first person said "Good luck" to Eddie midway through the day, he wondered what the kid was talking about. When the second kid said it, he knew. Apparently the word was out. By Friday they would be panting for action. The crowd would be huge indeed.

More than the words, Eddie felt the eyes. They were no longer only nickelhead eyes. They watched him in the hallways, the classrooms.

Heads turned. Voices whispered.

It was one thing to count yourself a goner. It was something else to have others agree. The funeral, it seemed, had already begun.

No matter how hard he tried to avoid Angelpuss, she always found him at least once a day, always cooing at him, no matter how many people were around. "Eddie, do the funky pickle once. Come on. Just for me?"

After school Eddie did not meet the Picklebus. He walked the streets of Cedar Grove. As far as he knew, he wasn't heading anywhere in particular, just wandering. Yet in fact something deep within was steering him, guiding him back to a place of happier times, of days that glowed like morning window shades. He turned a corner and walked no more. He was at Brockhurst Elementary, his old school.

His eyes watered up. The playground was nearly deserted, just a few little kids on the swings. How many recesses had he raced and screamed away on that playground?

He worked up his nerve and went inside. The hallways were empty. He peeked into one room, another. Empty. From somewhere came the sound of laughter. For an instant he thought he recognized the voice. Could it possibly be Mrs. Lewis?

Oh, how he had loved her! Once, on a note on his report card, she had called him my little ray of sunshine. If only she knew what can happen to little rays when they reach middle school.

He found his old second-grade room. He went in, looked around. He giggled out loud — there was the Child of the Day button, big as an all-day lollipop. How proud he had been to wear that giant yellow button when he was Child of the Day.

Eddie picked up a piece of chalk and wrote on the blackboard:

Dear Mrs. Lewis,
You are the best teacher I ever had.
A Former Student

He wiped his cheeks dry and went outside. The little kids were gone. He sat on a swing. It seemed so small now, he wondered if he would break it. He felt a little foolish, but he didn't care. He pushed off slightly, swinging just slightly back and forth, dragging his sneaker heels. In second grade he had needed to straighten his legs to touch the ground. He pushed off a little harder, then harder, and he felt that flying feeling and he knew then, no, it would not break, and so he went on swinging and swinging.

22

Sitting in homeroom Wednesday morning, Salem knew this was the day. The electronic three-note intro to the intercom announcements speared her breath. Her eyes fixed on the square charcoal speaker above the blackboard, she heard Principal Brimlow blather on about tryouts for this and practice for that and sign-ups for this and Parents' Night and teachers' in-service and keeping the lavatories clean and bringing a note from the doctor when you're absent for three days or more.

And then he talked about the visit of "one of your favorite authors and mine, Miss Willow Wembley." He talked about what an inspiration she was to kids all over the country. He charged everybody, "students and faculty alike, to be on our best behavior." He told everyone (for the millionth time) that Plumstead was a brand-new school, whose doors first opened in September, and therefore this was "an historic occasion" because Miss Wembley would be the first famous person ever to visit the school. "So let's show her," he practically yelled, "what it means to be the Plumstead Fighting Hamsters!"

Silence then. Is that all? feared Salem.

"And now," resumed the voice in the charcoal box, "the announcement you've all been waiting for. The results of the story-writing contest to determine who will personally escort Miss Wembley around the school on Friday." There was a pause, a rustle of paper. "May I have the envelope, please . . . ha-ha . . . just kidding, Hamsters. Okay, three winners, one from each grade . . . from grade six, Miss Wembley's personal escort will be . . . Dennis Johnson . . ."

Salem did not hear the rest of the announcement. She sat in numbed, stunned stillness. When her mind returned, it came in fragments.

Pickles.

Pickles?

Did I hear right?

Did he make a mistake?

Pickles?

There *must* be a mistake.

Pickles?

On the way to first class, Salem stopped by the main office. "May I see Mr. Brimlow?" she asked the secretary, Mrs. Wilburham.

Mrs. Wilburham, ever protective of her principal, asked in return, "What would you like to see him about?"

Salem's tongue felt dusty. "I . . . uh . . . just wanted to ask him something about one of the announcements today."

"And what — " Mrs. Wilburham was saying when Mr. Brimlow himself came out. His usual beaming face changed the instant he laid eyes on Salem. He knew very well of Salem's ambition to write, and the change in his face, slight as it was, gave Salem her answer: There had been no mistake. He was raising his hand to his red bow tie and opening his mouth to speak as Salem fled the office.

Later, in English, kids were mobbing Pickles, congratulating him. Through a thicket of back-slapping hands he looked her way, a funny smile on his face. Salem turned away.

When the bell ended class, Miss Comstock asked Pickles to stay for a minute.

After school Eddie visited Humphrey in the hamster tank in the lobby. Sunny was cleaning the tank and feeding the furry Plumstead mascot.

Watching the tiny brown rascal, Eddie fervently wished he were a hamster. "I'll bet Humphrey is the only one not at the fight," he said.

"What fight?" said Sunny, pushing the salt wheel under Humphrey's nose.

Eddie was shocked. "My fight. Friday."

Sunny shrugged indifferently. "Oh, that one." She carried the water bottle off for a refill.

Eddie couldn't believe it. Pickles had been acting the same way, saying things like, "Don't worry" and "No sweat." How could two of his best friends be so casual at a time like this?

When Sunny returned with a full bottle, he said, "Well you *are* going to be there, aren't you?"

Fixing the bottle to the glass wall of the tank, Sunny replied lazily, "Oh, probably not. I got stuff to do that day."

Meanwhile, four blocks from school, Pickles coasted his green six-wheeler alongside Salem. "I waited for you outside school," he said. "Give you a ride?"

Salem kept walking, her eyes straight ahead. "I'm fine."

"Come on, hop on."

"I said I'm fine."

Pickles coasted with her past several houses. "Where's your writing scarf?"

Salem stopped cold. She glared. "You're not funny."

Pickles spread his arms. "Who's trying to be funny?"

"You're rubbing it in. It's not enough that you won, now you're rubbing my face in it." She marched on.

Pickles caught up. "I'm sorry. I wasn't trying to rub it in. I wasn't even trying to win."

"Right." Even as Salem scoffed, she knew he was telling the truth. Pickles seldom tried to win at anything. He just did things because he felt like it. First or last never seemed to mean much to him, which made his victory in this case all the harder to take.

"Really," said Pickles. "You were right, it was just an assignment to me. Beginner's luck. What do I want with Willow Wembley?"

Salem picked up her pace. The wheels of the Picklebus hummed higher. Her eyes were stinging. She felt like screaming a million things. "Just leave me alone," she said.

He stopped. He let her walk another ten feet. Then he said, "Salem, I told Miss Comstock I didn't want to be an escort. She said if I really meant it, I should ask you if you would like to. Your story was next best."

Salem continued on several more steps. She stopped and turned. She leaned as if into a wind and screamed, "I am *not* anybody's *substitute!*"

For Eddie, this night was the worst yet. His nerves totally got the best of him. At dinner, he buried his burger in an avalanche of catsup. When he brushed his teeth, the toothbrush slipped out of his mouth and smeared his cheek with Colgate. Steering his feet into the leg holes of his pajamas

116

was like trying to thread a needle. He finally accomplished it only to discover that he had put them on backward.

He checked over his will. He had left most of his worldly possessions to his parents. There was something for each of his grandparents. Finally there was Pickles, Sunny, and Salem. The fact that Pickles and Sunny were taking his tragedy so lightly and Salem was ignoring him did not change the more enduring fact that they were his best friends in all the world.

To Pickles he had bequeathed his baseball glove and his pocket knife featuring a corkscrew and a tiny pair of tweezers. Tonight, that didn't seem enough to leave the very best of his best friends. So he threw in his lifetime collection of pennies, gathered from sidewalks, gutters, and floors in every corner of town. There was something special about a penny found. He never spent one. A hundred and twenty-one of them in the stomach of a fat glass frog on his dresser.

To Salem, the writer, he left the silver ballpoint pen he had received for Christmas and had never used.

To Sunny, after much thought, he had given maybe his most prized possession of all: the original eight-by-ten glossy print of a photograph from last summer. It showed him crossing first base in a Little League game, the first baseman stretching to receive the throw, the umpire calling him out. The picture had appeared next day on the front sports page of the Cedar Grove *Gazette*.

Eddie added one final item to his will — a tennis ball for Humphrey the hamster — and sealed it in an envelope. He placed it in the top drawer of his dresser, beneath his stack of undershirts.

He went to bed then, but not to sleep. Even leaving the bedside lamp turned on did not calm his nerves. At 11 o'clock he was still awake. At 11:05 a small smile appeared on his face, then a grin, then an ear-to-ear beamer. He had just thought of something. He could live to see Saturday after all. All he had to do was fake a stomachache on Friday morning. His mother would call him in sick. Edward Mott, absent.

Yeah!

He leapt to his dresser, tore up the will, and let the pieces snow into the wastebasket. He turned out the light and went straight to sleep.

23

When Pickles got to English class next day, he found a scrap of paper on his desk, folded four times. He unfolded it. It was a note. A short note.

> *OK*
> *S.*

Pickles glanced over to Salem's desk. She was sitting erect, staring straight ahead. He put the note in his pocket. He smiled to himself.

At her desk two aisles away, Salem clung fiercely to what little self-respect she had left. A night of dilemma had led her to a simple question: How will I feel the rest of my life knowing I blew my only chance to spend a day with Willow Wembley?

End of dilemma.

Halfway through class she risked a quick peek at Pickles. He was giving Miss Comstock his full attention. There was one thing Salem felt good about. She knew Pickles would not gloat, would never remind her that she had reversed herself. Some day she would thank him. But not today.

In the same class, while Miss Comstock read the final chapter of *The Owl Hoo Came to Dinner*, Eddie rewrote his will from memory.

By the time he had stepped off the school bus that morning, he had come to realize that he would not stay in bed tomorrow. It was not that he had changed his mind, for his mind still told him "be sick, be sick." No, there was something else inside him, something that had shouldered aside his common sense and commandeered his steering wheel. It ignored the notes found daily on his front door, this morning's saying "ONE MORE DAY." Whatever it was, it certainly hadn't been around when the bully chased him from the basketball court. As far as Eddie could tell, this something else was stupid and useless. It had done nothing more than leave him back where he had started: scared stiff.

It had taken Salem till the end of classes to work up the nerve to say something. She came up behind Sunny at her locker. "Did you hear what Pickles did?"

Sunny turned. She raised her eyebrows. "Well, well, it speaks."

Salem glared. "Okay, so I get wrapped up sometimes. Are you going to answer my question?"

Sunny shut her locker door. "He won the contest. That what you mean?" She gave Salem a funny look, then started down the hallway. "Gotta feed Humphrey."

Walking along, Salem said, "He told Miss Comstock he doesn't want to escort Willow Wembley. He said I should."

Sunny stopped. "So? Are you?" Again she looked at Salem funny.

Salem nodded. "I guess so." Sunny started walking. "What do you think?"

"I think that's pretty nice of him, is what I think."

Salem smiled fondly. "I think so, too."

When they reached Humphrey's tank, Sunny turned to Salem and stared at her. "What's that on your neck?"

Eddie had never been so aware of time. Each minute that blinked from the red LED display on his clock seemed to reel him in closer to the gallows.

He went to the window, looked out at the moon. For the last time? he wondered. He turned out his light so he could see outside better. The moon seemed to have a calming effect on him, seemed to beckon him into the vastness of a future in which the next twenty-four hours were a mere blip. He began to see himself immortalized. Perhaps they would change the name of his old school to Edward A. Mott Elementary. They did things like that when kids died. Or name a street after him. Or a cupcake. He could see his tearful mother saying to reporters, "Oh, how he used to love those cupcakes."

The mood lasted only as long as he looked out the window. Turning back to the room, he felt nothing but a black and immense loneliness. He turned the light back on.

He knew he needed help to make it through the night. He found it in a corner of his closet, in the old computer paper box that held his father's collection of Bugs Bunny comic books. He brought them out, he laid them on the bed, and for hours he giggled at Bugs and Yosemite Sam and Elmer Fudd, and he could not remember ever being so happy in his life.

24

"CHICKEN POX?" Salem shrieked. "I *can't* have chicken pox!"

"You can," her mother replied evenly, "and you do."

Salem looked again at her red-speckled stomach. She yanked down her pajama top. "Well that's too bad. I'm going to school." She got up from her bed.

Her mother stood directly in front of her. "Lie. . . . Down."

"Mom, I *have* to go to school."

"You're not going anywhere. You're sick. Lie down."

"Mom, this is the day I escort Willow Wembley."

"She'll have to manage without you."

Salem implored, "This is the biggest day of my entire *life*. My *career* is at stake."

"Your heinie's going to be at stake if you don't lie down."

Salem gaped unbelievingly into her mother's face and saw that she would never win. She threw herself onto the bed. With both hands she pounded her pillow. She rolled into a fetal position, clutching her pajamas and wailing in agony.

Eddie took unusual care in dressing and grooming himself that morning. It had occurred to him that if he were destined to be laid out in an emergency ward sometime after school, with doctors and nurses peeling off his clothes and searching for a pulse, well, he had better be presentable. So he took extra time brushing his teeth, dug out dirt from under his fingernails, rubbed his father's deodorant all over his body, and picked out his cleanest, newest underwear.

After breakfast he went upstairs to touch his old Daffy Duck pin for the last time. Back downstairs, he kissed both his mother and father — something he hadn't done in a long time — and left them gawking and speechless when he said, "You were the best mom and dad a kid could ever have." He then gave them what he hoped would be remembered as a brave little smile and departed.

Sunny and Pickles were on his doorstep. Pickles had a briefcase.

"What are you doing here?"

Pickles tapped the long green six-wheeler with

his green sneaker toe. "Figured you should go to school in style."

Just the way Pickles said it, and the way Sunny looked at him, Eddie knew he had been wrong. They *were* concerned, they *did* care. They just acted as if they didn't.

The three of them boarded the Picklebus and pushed off. Eddie glanced back at his front door. There was no note. He guessed that if he searched his fellow riders, he would find a crumpled piece of paper in one of their pockets.

As they rolled along toward school, he realized that even their arrangement on the board — Pickles in front, Sunny behind, himself in the middle — was no accident. He was the ham in a loving sandwich.

Thanks to the visit by Willow Wembley, every student at Plumstead got out of at least one class. There were three assemblies in the auditorium, for the eighth-, the seventh-, and finally the sixth-graders.

In the last period, the author also conducted a workshop for those especially interested in writing. After each session she autographed copies of her books, not to mention a few backs of hands and one plaster cast. She survived lunch in the cafeteria with the students, an interview with the editor of the school newspaper, and her sixth-grade escort — an awestruck, practically hysterical girl — who at one point ushered her into a broom closet.

Eddie drifted on the currents of the day. There was little sense of time or place, only a vague wandering as if in a liquid dream. Faces floated by like jellyfish.

One belonged to the famous visiting author, Willow Wembley. Eddie saw her once breezing by in the hallway, once at lunch, and of course on the auditorium stage. She dressed a lot like Salem, especially the long skirt. Eddie had expected gray hair, but hers was brown, again reminding him of Salem.

But she was different from Salem, too. She seemed very open and chummy, chatting and laughing and even horseplaying with the students. Except for her size, she would have made a pretty good sixth-grader. Salem, too, could be chummy and even goofy, but only her close friends saw that side of her. To most others, she often appeared more grown-up than kid. In the lunchroom someone gave Willow Wembley a FIGHTING HAMSTERS T-shirt. To the cheers of the students, she pulled it right on over her blouse.

From the moment Willow Wembley arrived that morning, there was an awareness of her presence throughout the school, a sense of something special, a constant buzz of excitement shared by students and teachers alike. There was also a second, competing buzz, this one sensed only by the students, felt as a tremor in the bones that dove-tailed by noon into the midsection, crept up the windpipe and, at precisely 2:35, the end of school, erupted from a hundred adolescent tongues:

"FIIIIIIIGHT!"

Eddie put all his books in his locker, plus his looseleaf and pencils. Everything. For once, no books to carry home. He hadn't bothered to write down his homework assignments. He closed his locker and spun the combination. They would have to saw it open.

He started down the hallway. Before he had taken five steps he was joined by several class-mates. Rounding the corner, he picked up more. By the time he reached the door, he was the eye of a swirling gale, calling:

"Get 'im, Eddie!"

"Show him the funky punch!"

"Go, Mott!"

Eddie heard them only as background static. While his legs carried him numbly forward, his mind ferried him back to playground days at Brockhurst, to birthday parties, and Saturday morning cartoons. Eddie was back at his favorite birthday party of all time, the one at Dumbo's with five of his friends, kicking off their shoes and diving into the fat, red, billowing, air-filled mat-tress and laughing and jumping and screaming and jumping. He found himself alone, the mob peeling away. And before him, arms folded, scowling, was Weasel Munshak.

In the first rank of the encircling crowd was Angelpuss, her mouth open, her eyes wide, her orange hair spike looking taller than ever, as if growing with excitement. Eddie did not see Pickles, or Sunny, or Salem. In fact, he hadn't seen Salem all day. Apparently she wanted no part of a gladiator on his day at the Colosseum.

Eddie wondered where he was, where had the mob led him. He looked around, but all he could see above the heads of the crowd was blue sky. When his eyes returned to earth, he found Weasel extending his arm, crooking his index finger, wagging it: Come on. Eddie just stood there, looking, blinking. Weasel wagged. Eddie stood.

Weasel stepped forward. Girls screamed. Boys laughed at the girls, some making mock, falsetto screams of their own.

Another step.

The crowd went bonkers. The gap was now five feet. Eddie could have taken one step and scratched Weasel's nose.

Another step . . . and above the bonkers, splitting it like a spiked shaft, a scream so dazzling that it froze every movement, every breath. Weasel's eyes shifted, his head turned. Eddie didn't have to turn. He was already looking at the right place, past Weasel's polka-dotted hairdo to Angelpuss, her mouth still open, the moussy glop of her orange spike firmly in the grip of Pickles' right hand. On the other side of her stood Sunny. Sunny's arms were raised. She held a pair of hedge clippers. The open blades of the clippers formed a V, with the orange spike between them.

In the cold stone silence, Pickles leaned in to Angelpuss's ear. He appeared to whisper something. He pulled away.

Angelpuss screeched. "Don't touch him!"

Pickles leaned in again to whisper. The clippers were poised between the top of Angelpuss's scalp and Pickles' hand.

"I was just messing around. To make you jealous!"

Pickles whispered.

"I don't like him! I never liked him! He's a jerk!"

Pickles whispered.

"A little twerp!"

Another whisper, longer this time.

"If you touch him they're gonna cut my hair off! They *will*! They'll do it! Don't *ever* touch him! Or they'll find me and do it!"

One last whisper.

"In my *sleep*!"

Weasel took a long time to turn back to Eddie. He looked him up and down. He gave a sneering grin and walked away.

25

When the bedside clock turned to 2:35, Salem groaned and scratched and buried her face in the pillow. "It's over . . . it's ooooover." All day long, hour by hour, she had been picturing what she would be doing had she been in school.

Every five minutes she had lifted her pajama top to check her stomach, hoping each time to find that a miracle had occurred, that the red dots were gone, and she would leap from bed and be at school in five minutes flat. Now, not even a miracle would help. The opportunity of a lifetime: gone, poof.

A mere week ago the future had been so bright with promise. Since then she had lost the story contest, missed a day with Willow Wembley, mistreated Eddie, alienated Sunny and Pickles, and caught the chicken pox. Could life get any worse? She had read that great literature often comes out of great tragedy. If that was true, well, Shakespeare better move over.

In the meantime she buried her face deeper in

the pillow and scratched and groaned some more. It was about a half hour later when she heard the doorbell ring. Her mother answered . . . voices . . . the door closing . . . footsteps on the stairs . . . one voice, a man's, familiar. ". . . heard she was absent . . ." Mr. Brimlow! Salem sat up, stuffed the pillow behind her, scratched. Wasn't that nice of him. He knew how devastated she was.

The door opened, her mother's face appeared. Her eyes were twinkling. "Salem, someone to see you."

Salem forced a smile, for her principal's sake. "Okay."

Her mother stepped aside for the visitor. It wasn't Mr. Brimlow. It was someone Salem had seen a thousand times on the dust covers of a dozen novels. *Willow Wembley!*"

Beaming as if greeting a long-lost daughter, Willow Wembley strode straight for the bed, hand extended. "Salem Brownmiller, I presume? The young author?"

Salem could not move except to repeat hoarsely, "Willow Wembley."

The great author laughed. "Don't wear it out." She grabbed Salem's hand and shook it. She sat on the bed, holding Salem's hand in both of hers, smiling in a way she never did on her dust covers. "I'm sorry I missed you today."

Salem blurted, "I have the chicken pox!" And

then she was sobbing against Willow Wembley's shoulder, wrapped in the author's arms.

"I know, I know. I remember when I had them. They just ruin one's life, don't they?"

Salem pulled back, amazed at the author's insight. "They *do!*"

"Yes, but only until Doctor Wembley shows up. Thanks to Mr. Brimlow. Aren't you glad you have a principal who cares so much?"

Mr. Brimlow grinned sheepishly and waved from the foot of the bed.

"Thank you, Mr. Brimlow."

Miss Wembley stood and looked around. "Left Bank, huh?" She nodded approvingly. "Well, I'm *wearing* my inspiration." She spread her jacket. "Like it?"

The elegant, the exquisite Willow Wembley was wearing a FIGHTING HAMSTERS T-shirt. Salem nodded, incredulous.

The author fished into her shoulder bag. "It should be here . . . somewhere . . . ah!" She pulled out a thin black ballpoint pen. "In my motel room last night, I wrote a couple pages of the next Klatterfield book, with this." She held out the pen. "Would you like to have it?"

Salem wanted to cry. "Oh, thank you." She cradled the pen lovingly in both hands, then was seized by an itching fit. Her frenzied scratching brought laughter from everyone, including herself.

"My mother put washcloths dipped in tea on me," said Willow Wembley. "Didn't stop the itch, but I got a great tan!"

Gales of laughter filled the room. In the lull that followed, Salem's voice came timidly. "Miss Wembley?"

The author turned to her the gentlest face she had ever seen. "Yes?"

"Miss Wembley, I just . . . I . . . can't believe you're really here. I mean, you're so busy writing books and all."

The author smiled. She stroked Salem's cheek. "Yes, writing is important, but people are more important." She lightly pressed the end of Salem's nose. "Don't you agree?"

Salem hesitated.

The doorbell rang. Mrs. Brownmiller hurried downstairs, and moments later Sunny, Pickles, and Eddie burst into the room.

Only now, seeing Eddie, did Salem realize how much she had feared for his safety. "You're okay," she marveled. "What happened?"

Her three friends laughed. Pickles patted a large briefcase he was carrying. "It's a long story."

"Put it this way," said Eddie, wincing, "I'll never do the funky pickle again."

Salem turned to Willow Wembley. "The answer," she said firmly, "is yes."

About the Author

Jerry Spinelli was born in Norristown, Pennsylvania. He attended Gettysburg College and The Writing Seminars at Johns Hopkins University. His novels include *Maniac Magee,* which won the Newbery Medal; *Fourth Grade Rats*; and *Report to the Principal's Office* and *Who Ran My Underwear Up the Flagpole?*, the first two books in the School Daze series. He lives in Phoenixville, Pennsylvania, with his wife and fellow author, Eileen Spinelli, and sons, Sean and Ben.

If chilling out is your favorite thing to do, you'll love